# She Didn't Say No

by

# Charmaine Gordon

Vanilla Heart Publishing

**She Didn't Say No**
by Charmaine Gordon

Copyright 2014 Charmaine Gordon

Published by: Vanilla Heart Publishing
www.VanillaHeartBookAndAuthors.com
10121 Evergreen Way, 25-156
Everett, WA 98204 USA

This book is a work of fiction. Names, characters, places, and incidents are either the product of the author's imagination or are used fictitiously, and any resemblance to places, events, or persons living or dead is purely coincidental.

ISBN-13: 978-0615959863  ISBN-10: 0615959865

10 9 8 7 6 5 4 3 2 1 First Edition

First Printing, February 2014
Printed in the United States of America

# She Didn't Say No

by

Charmaine Gordon

# Table of Contents

# Dedication

*She Didn't Say No* could not have been written without the help from my daughter, Amy Malone. With patience and care, she researched and answered my questions the way I've done for her in all our precious years together. This is not the first time Amy sorted out a story with me and it won't be the last. Thank you, my one and only daughter. This story is for you. Love, Mom

# Acknowledgements

Thanks to Kimberlee Williams, the best publisher ever, for her encouragement to this less than computer savvy author.

If you listen to words of wisdom and follow the lead, you can't go wrong. Thanks for support and friendship to said Ms. Williams and to Chelle Cordero, always there with a helping hand. And to Angela Kay Austin who listened to me when we first met, I'm happy we've remained close friends.

# Chapter One
# 1960. A year full of promise

I focused on studies; my goal to be a veterinarian required concentration and high grades. The library emptied most Saturday afternoons as the campus prepared for dates, parties and events that had nothing to do with me, a country girl from way upstate New York with ambition and parent's expectations of greatness from their only child. One student, I'd seen him before, a guy called a BMOC, Big Man On Campus, glanced over from another table and grinned.

"Hey, you. I've seen you a bunch of times before with your cute little nose in the books. Don't you ever come up for air?"

*Me? He spoke to me? This handsome guy, captain of the swim team said my nose is cute.*

Next thing I knew, he plunked books next to me and grinned again.

"Scott Dwyer." He extended his right hand, muscles rippling through his white tee shirt.

I tentatively reached over to shake it and he pulled me closer. "Don't be afraid. I don't bite."

Grasping his hand with a firm grip, I shook it. "I'm not afraid of anything. I'm Grace Meredith. Now I must finish this chapter before the library closes."

"What's your goal, Miss big brain. You're young to be graduating this year. How did that happen? Did Daddy pay off someone?"

I stiffened, wanting to smack his face. "Hey, not that it's any of your business but I've been an accelerated student all the way through school and I've earned my way to graduate by studying."

Hey, Grace, I'm sorry. I'm not stupid even if I am a jock. I heard you were nineteen and I had to meet you for a lot of reasons."

Curious, I wanted to hear the reasons why the BMOC even thought about me at all. "Reasons?"

He tilted his head, a blond curl fell across his forehead. Counting on his fingers, he held up a thumb. "Number one—you're different from the other girls, not flirty and teasing all the time. Number two—you have a style all your own and I admire that. Number three."

"Stop. You're embarrassing me." I wanted to hear more words pour from this handsome boy who made me mad and now I liked him.

He grinned. "So what's your goal with all this," he gestured to the heap of books on the table, "all this uh, studying?"

"I plan to be a veterinarian. How about you?"

"Law with a strong leaning toward criminal justice."

"Like FBI or Police Academy?"

He frowned. "Not sure. It's all so far away but maybe I'll specialize in the K-9 Corp. See, we both care about animals. We have something in common."

He sat back and appeared to be very pleased with himself. I liked his self confidence, something I lacked even though I'd boasted about not being afraid of anything. *Right.* My parents frightened me with their expectations and pressure. A buzzer sounded signaling time's up at the library. I slammed the book shut and jumped to my feet. "Scott, how about playing hooky from studying and let's go to the beach."

Did I catch a surprised look on his handsome face? "I'm with you, Grace. Just so happens I have a car."

"Oh." I blushed. I hadn't thought about getting there. Today I'd walked from my small apartment close to campus. "Cool." And we were off on a late spring afternoon in 1960 driving in a shiny yellow Volkswagen Bug.

He zoomed down the road laughing when the scarf I'd tied over my hair blew off and landed in the back. "Your hair is pretty blowing around in the wind."

*So this is what it's like being with a guy,* I thought. *Having fun and a little flirting. He sure had experience talking. He's the pretty one, not me.*

We went to Nyack about a half hour north of school and parked at the hiking section. "There's a small beach a little way up over some boulders. The Hudson River is darn cold right now but beautiful." He gave me another half grin, grabbed a blanket from the trunk and we climbed a short way.

Goose bumps rose on my arms from the breeze blowing across the water. No jacket and I'm shaking. What an impression to make on this guy. And suddenly Scott wrapped his arms and the blanket around us and we were all alone. Body heat warmed and overwhelmed me with a yearning I'd never experienced before.

"Better?" His voice had deepened. He rubbed my arms.

"Yes. Much better. I should've worn a jacket."

The kiss, tentative at first, made me tingle all over. I'd never had a boyfriend before. This feeling was new to me. Too busy being the obedient daughter appeasing my parents demands on time to experiment at being a kid, a teenager. So here I am at nineteen not knowing what to do with a first kiss, for God sake.

"Well, uh hi Scott. You're a um, good kisser."

Laughing, he hugged me tight. "Only good? I can do better than that." This time the kiss curled my socks and knocked me for a loop.

Gasping for breath, I yelled, "Bingo." The wind carried my word across the river and boomeranged back for an echo. "Bingo, bing, bin."

Sitting at the edge where sand meets water, sheltered by some boulders Scott asked me about my background. I said, "You first," certain he'd grown up in a house with a picket fence, smiling parents, siblings and lots of relatives. All true as his fairy tale life of twenty one years unfolded.

"I hope I didn't bore you, Grace." He planted a kiss on top of my straight brown hair. "Do you realize how pretty you are and the way your eyes match your hair? They're so dark and mysterious. Are secrets hiding behind there?"

Giggling, I nodded. "I'm nineteen. Never been kissed 'til you."

Frowning, he looked across the river and seemed to think about what I'd said.

"That's a big responsibility but I can handle it. Now tell me about your life."

Without meeting his eyes, I told him everything, how my parents ruled my life up in Buffalo, NY and allowed me to attend this school far southeast from them for the first time with high expectancy for success. So far so good since my grades were outstanding. Best of all I had money my sweet grandfather left in an account no one else could touch but me."

"Oh." Scott held me close and I pictured other girls cuddling up in his arms. "Tell me about your grandfather. I have both sets of grandparents still living. Lucky for me."

I had to smile at Scott's interest and told him of my stern grandfather who melted whenever he saw me. "Scott, we didn't have a big family like you do so the fact that my grandfather cared for me and showed he loved me and I could fly into his arms and he'd whirl me around and laugh was one of the few real joys growing up. Mother would try to stop him. He never listened."

"What did he do? I mean his work?"

"He was a banker who worked himself up to CEO and president and without telling my parents, made out his will leaving everything to me. His top financial advisor contacted me privately after the funeral and set up a plan where the money would grow and I'd be independently comfortable for the rest of my life."

"Wow. That's quite a story. Thanks for telling me." His arms went around me and I felt safe. "Let's have dinner somewhere close and head back to the campus. Okay?"

"Sure." I prayed he'd want to see me again, to hold and kiss me some more but first dinner. One step at a time, I cautioned. I had a few more years of school to get a veterinarian degree, probably at Purdue and he had major plans for his future. Right now, with his warm hand high on my thigh, I couldn't think clearly.

After burgers, fries, and milkshakes he followed my directions to my apartment. Looking up at the nice building, he smiled. "So you live here. I've passed this place like a zillion times never thinking the girl of my dreams might be right upstairs."

"Girl of your dreams?" I smacked his shoulder. "You probably say that to all the girls."

"No, Grace. I mean it. I've admired you for months at the library and here we are."

*Is this where I say come up or what?* And then I heard myself asking if he'd like to come up and we were inside and kissing in my quiet apartment where no one ever came. Ever until now. I always wondered what happens when two young people are alone, hormones raging. Hearing about it and reading books is not the same. I wore a spring sweater set, pleated skirt, underwear, socks and sneakers. Nothing sexy except my feelings and wanting him. Scott had experience on his side. Was I expected to be a casual lay? I didn't know and didn't care.

First we sat on the couch and necked. That led to touching and stroking each other and then , oh so politely, he asked if I minded if he did this and that and soon we were naked on my maiden double bed with pink flowered sheets and a matching spread.

"Grace, you're so beautiful." He fondled my breasts as if they were treasures and tasted one nipple and then the other. And sucked like a baby searching for milk. My hands grabbed his head, ran my fingers through his thick curly hair and held him close never wanting him to leave me. My first lover. My only love. "Do you have protection?" *Protection? Um, oh birth control.*

"I have a diaphragm and cream but I never used it." It occurred to me this was a funny conversation in the heat of nakedness.

"Oh. Well, this time leave it up to me. Next time practice until you get it right because I have a feeling we're gonna need a lot of protection." He groaned and I heard a rip of a packet and fumbling and soon he played with the dark moist space between my thighs until I lifted my hips to heaven. Slowly, he entered the virgin territory where only a tampon had been. No comparison here as he continued to move in a little deeper each time to break the barrier and we were one reaching for the stars.

*So this is what all the fuss is all about*, I thought. And I wanted more and right away. Like a demon possessed, I coaxed his wilted member into an upright position after about half an hour and we lost count by night's end collapsing in each other's arms.

Vowing to love each other forever, finish school in a few years and begin a life together, we became the hottest unlikely new couple on campus. The studious girl and the BMOC. School first the priority. We made a promise not to interfere with our different plans. I'd be off to Purdue and he hadn't solidified his plans yet. Law schools offered scholarships for the brightest students; pick one. He'd almost made up his mind since graduation was in June, a couple of months away.

A month later I missed my period. Always on time, first I worried and kept it to myself and then frantic, I told him a big fat lie. Crossing my fingers and hoping to die for what I was about to say, I called my dearest love. "I'm sick with the flu and don't want you to catch it." Busy with finals, Scott said okay and he missed me and hoped I felt better soon and we'd be together again. I sniffled and said yes to my first and only love.

By the second late period, I was sure. Skipping classes and having someone bring assignments to my apartment, I completed my work. Making a list of pros and cons, I faced the facts. By now, I'd cried too much pacing the floor alone with no one to talk to and afraid I might hurt the baby with all my grief, I reached for an inner strength to move on. Heartbroken, the practical side of me decided Scott must never know. I couldn't burden his life, ruin his career with a baby. As for me, I'd go to Buffalo, tell my parents and they'd help me solve the problem.

My dearest Scott. Tears fell. Ink ran. I started over many times until the well ran dry, crumpled paper littered the floor and I wrote:

My Dearest Scott,

I'm saying goodbye. Not because I want to but because I have to. Our paths are too divergent to survive the long wait until we can be together. You must go your way and I have to go mine. Please know you are my one and only love. I wish you well. Have a good life. And, and I don't know what else to say except goodbye.

19

Grace.

The letter made no sense. Choices made with no guidance. Choices that changed our lives forever.

Packing all my belongings including books, I gazed around the only place I'd found love and happiness for a short time. I made the long drive from St. Thomas Aquinas University up to Buffalo in a new two door Pontiac I'd bought a few days ago, my first car thanks to my generous grandfather. All the way northwest I thought about the baby. Above all I want her or him to feel peaceful and calm. I won't let anyone stand in the way of my baby's happiness. Naïve when I think back.

Gutsy and determined I parked in the driveway of the home I'd grown up in. *No joy here*, I thought, *but surely my parents would help sort this serious situation out for me, their only daughter*. I opened the door with my own key and called, "Mother, are you home?"

"Grace, what are you doing here?" She took one look at my loose jeans and tee shirt and stepped back.

I could tell. She knew. Her lips tightened in a thin line. It was a 'wait until your father hears about this' moment. How dumb to come home. They wouldn't open their closed hearts. I'd disappointed them. About to shame them to their friends and now they would hate me. I heard the silent accusatory words in my mind. "We'll never be able to hold up our heads in the community or in church if word gets out you're pregnant. Abortion or go away and give the baby up for adoption." Parents are supposed to guide their kids and I need help right now.


Without a word, I left. I wiped sweaty hands dry on a loose tee shirt and drove, and finally stopped at what appeared to be a well kept small town. A wide street with no debris blowing around and aromas coming from Betty's Home Cookin' Diner. The diner smelled of home cooked food as advertised. Hungry, I ordered vegetable soup and toast, nibbling on crackers until a steaming bowl arrived. Plans. I had to make plans for our future. Listening in on conversations around me, I hear two girls talking about a Dr. Feldman who delivered so and so's baby and what a great guy blah, blah, blah. My ears perked up and I scribbled his name on a paper napkin. Using the phone booth outside, I called his number to speak with the secretary. A kind deep voice answered.

"Hi. I just came to town and need to see Dr. Feldman right away. Is he in like now?"

"I'm Dr. Feldman and yes I'm here. What seems to be the problem? Can you wait until office hours tomorrow?"

"Oh." I wanted to cry. He sounded so nice and , and uh, patient. "Sir, it can't wait. I can't wait. Please."

He gave me directions and I drove to his office at the back of a house with a white picket fence, purple hydrangeas in bloom and a bed of all colors of tulips just like the ones Scott had described about the house he's grown up in. So warm and homey. I rang the bell and heard the bark of a large dog respond.

"Now Maggie, we have a young lady visitor. Be a good girl." Dr Feldman greeted me with a warm smile, a white female sheep dog with short clipped hair stood at his side. "Are you afraid of dogs?"

"Oh no. I wanted to be a veterinarian and now I think my plans will have to change." I held out my hand and Maggie sniffed. I pointed down. She hunkered down. I signaled stay. She stayed.

"Impressive. Obviously you've had a lot of training or you've studied hard." I nodded. "The reason for your call is not about dogs, I assume."

21

"Yes sir. I think, I know I'm pregnant and I hope you'll confirm it."

"Why me?"

I searched for an answer by checking out his diplomas and pictures. Finally I spilled the beans. "No one knows. My boyfriend loves me but we, well he has a few years of law school ahead and I can't burden him with a baby so I didn't tell him. Maybe it's wrong of me to decide for him but he's a good guy. He'd say yes and throw away his future. My parents turned their backs on me so I'm going to have my baby and raise her or him by myself. And that's what my plan is."

We looked at each other for a long time. "If you don't want to help me, I'll drive 'til I find another doctor." Standing, I picked up my bag. Maggie stood too and got in my way.

"She's herding you. That's what she does. Do you mind telling me your name?"

*Should I lie? What if there was an APB out for me?* "Grace."

"Grace, if you were my daughter, I'd give you different advice but since your mind is made up, for now, let's have a look to make sure. It's the very least I can do.

After the examination, I dressed and met Dr. Feldman in his office. His smile seemed sad. "Yes, you're about eleven weeks pregnant. I have a bottle of pre natal vitamins here for you. Take one a day and when you get settled, find an obstetrician. Meanwhile," he handed a paper to me, "here's a good diet to follow. Eat healthy, low fat foods, low calorie, veggies, fruits, juice. In other words, follow this diet. You won't regret it." He walked me to the door. "Take this card and don't lose it. If you need advice, change your mind, or just want to say Happy New Year, please do."

I knew we'd never meet again.

"I know you're not coming back, young lady" He patted my hand. "Whatever it is you're running from, find roots in a thriving town and start fresh. I have a good feeling about you. I'd truly like to see a Christmas card from you every year. Drop a line to say you're feeling fine."

I left not wanting to shed a tear and hit the road after swallowing a vitamin with water from a fountain in the park across the street. While having the tank filled before I left the town, I asked for a map of New York State. The filling station wasn't busy and the owner came out to chat.

"What're you looking for?"

He had the feel of a man who'd been there forever but it turned out he'd come up northwest from Brooklyn to find peace in the country.

"I want a nice town to start a pet grooming business." *Where did that come from?* I wondered. *Veterinarian dreams already faded to a simpler more manageable kind of business yet I'd still be with dogs and cats. Yes I'd have a lot to learn but I recalled you could learn the how-to as an apprentice or take classes for certification.* My mind worked faster than my mouth just then. "In your travels, did you ever come across towns you thought might be appropriate for a person starting out on her own?"

He stuck out a hand for me to shake. "Jack Connor, here. All alone, huh?"

I shook his hand and shrugged. "Tired of college and being bossed around by the folks back home. Callie Feld." The name popped out so I went with it.

"Well Callie, there's a nice area of towns where there's waterfalls 'n creeks not far from Rockland County. Just far enough to be real pretty and small townish, if ya know what I mean. One I always liked is River's Edge. You might check that out. See if they have pet groomers there. I settled here 'cause my wife wanted to be near her people. It's been good for us and the kids."

## She Didn't Say No

He made some marks on the map circling the area. I thanked my helpful new friend, Jack, paid the bill and drove on. Breathing deeply, thankful for kind people, I let go of anger toward parents who had no time to care for or understand me.

# Chapter Two
# Moving on

The kindness of strangers along the way. That's what helped me on the path to my new home. Nineteen and pregnant but I had money enough to make a good start for us. I found the town and there were no pet grooming businesses nearby. Without much trouble, I smiled my way into a realtor's office and told the receptionist what I needed. With a skeptical look, she buzzed someone and after a few minutes, a gray haired tall man came out.

"I'm Jim Trumbull. Please come in."

*Uh oh. He's the boss. The company's name was Trumbull Realty. I needed to rev up my confidence factor and appear to be sure of myself. Well, I am confident, damn it.*

I smiled bright and sweet. "I'm new in town and I want to buy a place big enough to establish a pet grooming emporium with an apartment for me above or maybe behind the property."

He blinked a few times and polished his glasses. "Your name is?"

"Sorry." I grinned. "Grace Meredith."

"Miss Meredith, the property you request may be very costly. Do you have the means?"

"Do you have such a property, Mr. Trumbull? If so, I'd like to see it right away or you may have a few suitable for my specifications. Then we can discuss my means, as you call it."

He leaned back in his chair and laughed so hard his glasses fell off and clattered to the floor. Picking them up, he mopped his eyes dry with a handkerchief. "Let's go, young lady. I do believe I have the perfect place for you and your pet emporium.

Coincidence, karma, fate or all of the above brought me to River's Edge that day. I'd had enough bad luck in my life and now a new beginning. Mr. Trumbull drove me a few blocks from his office. We could have walked but I guessed this was the way he treated clients. A corner lot with a building loomed ahead. He parked. We got out. My heart beat faster as I surveyed what to my inexperienced eyes, appeared to be two lots with one cozy looking building constructed of natural wood not exactly a cabin; more like a big cottage.

*Don't appear to be too excited,* I thought. *I wanted to twirl around and dance. I couldn't negotiate a price if I showed eagerness so be cool, Grace. Let's see what's inside.*

"The owner, Doctor Daly, had a good veterinarian practice here for years. He retired a few months ago and moved to Florida. We all miss him. Let's go inside."

*It was a sign. Pets had been here. A veterinarian. I felt it in my bones and heart. Oh baby, this is the place.*

Doctor Daly left the place clean inside. I wandered around touching everything to picture what I'd need for my purpose. I climbed the stairs to follow Mr. Trumbull's lead. The apartment up there was plain, not meant to be a real living space but okay for now. Bathroom, small kitchen, again all clean. I'd need a good carpenter.

"Seen enough, Miss Meredith?"

"I'd like to check out the yard."

"Follow me and be careful."

A high pioneer fence guarded the yard with a dog run on one side and flower beds in bloom everywhere. An old majestic oak tree grew in one section.

"How much?" I couldn't help myself from asking.

Again he laughed hard enough to set birds flying. "You're supposed to play hard to get, Miss Meredith."

*Oh, Mr. Trumbull, that's how I got in trouble. I didn't say no soon enough.*

Grinning, I said, "It's perfect for me and my uh, business. Now we negotiate, right?"

Ever the gentleman, he took my arm to guide me through the yard, cottage and the front path back to his car. Instead of the office, he drove to a restaurant just outside of the town's limits. River's Edge Fine Dining. "This is the best restaurant for miles around. People come up from New York City to dine here."

A good looking man greeted Mr. Trumbull. A black Labrador Retriever stayed at his side secured by a lead. I offered my palm to the dog. He sniffed then licked with obvious enthusiasm.

"This is Grace Meredith, Larry. She's a dog person who intends to open a pet grooming emporium right here on Main Street." Mr. Trumbull introduced me to my first client before I had a shop or anything.

"Jim, you've brought Grace to the right restaurant. Dinner's on the house to welcome a soon to be member of the Chamber of Commerce. I'm Larry Owens, Grace. And this is my hunting dog and best pal, Spike."

"May I pet him?"

"You seem to know what you're doing. Go ahead."

"Come, Spike." I opened my hand. He took his time and approached.

"Good boy." I used the squeaky voice dogs love. Kneeling, I pointed to the ground. He sat and again lavished kisses enough to warm my heart. "Spike, you're the best."

Long strokes from head to tail sealed the deal. Spike and I bonded.

"Good show, Grace. Spike doesn't respond to strangers. There's a nice table outside in back so you can get your first look at the waterfalls we're known for."

Overcome by kindness and hospitality, I first went to the ladies room and washed up, added lip gloss to an otherwise pale face. Hungry and tired after the long journey from Buffalo and back I wondered what came next. *Pinch me if it all went well*, I thought and went outside.

Mr. Trumbull sat, a folder opened next to menus. Water cascaded to the rocks below creating an echo to bounce off the sides of huge boulders along the banks of a stream.

All of a sudden I felt small and too young and inexperienced to be a mother, a business person, a mother, a, well anyone except a student taking tests alone in a small apartment on a campus. I could end this charade, this pretense by throwing myself over the balcony onto the rocks. How foolish to run away and think I could raise a baby, start a business all by myself.

Mr. Trumbull's hand warmed mine. "Grace, speak to me. I'm a good listener."

The kindness of strangers. I told him my whole story. More than he needed to know. We had soup between little segments and by the time we had the main course of broiled salmon, so delicious with steamed spinach just like on Dr. Feldman's diet, I'd finished.

Patting his lips, he set the napkin aside. "We have a three-fold problem to solve. You need a good obstetrician and I know just the doctor right here in town and after the baby's born, you'll need. . ."

I gasped. My hands flew to my belly. "How did you know?"

He moved his chair closer. I hoped he didn't want our conversation to be overheard. "In order to be successful in my business, I learned long ago to study people. Every so often you stroke your tummy in a protective or soothing motion. I've seen this before and knew." He touched my hand. "You have nothing to fear from me, Grace. Try to keep calm and listen. Deal?"

"Okay. I'll try and it's a deal." I breathed in through my nose for an eight count, held for eight and exhaled through my mouth the way the best phys ed teacher ever taught my first year at college. After a few times, I calmed and listened as agreed. As he spoke, I recognized experience and authority in his voice.

"The Emporium must be fitted for your purpose and you'll need hired help. At least two capable experienced dog and cat lovers. You might want to begin with just dogs to keep it simple while the baby is young. And you will want to be a certified groomer to enhance your respectability. I'll help you check into that. And a number one priority is a proper apartment upstairs for you and yours." He rubbed his hands together, a smile tugging at the corners of his mouth.

"Sounds overwhelming. It is overwhelming. I must be nuts to think I'm capable of doing all this alone." Again I watched the waterfall pound away at the rocks wishing I could escape. *How did a simple life get so complicated? Choices, Grace. You made choices.*

"You don't have to, Grace. The past few years have proved to be shocking and ultimately left me bored. My son Ryan flew the coop and moved out west. My wife decided she didn't want to be married to boring James Trumbull, Realtor anymore and divorced me. And suddenly you marched into my life like a ray of sunshine with determination and guts to take on an impossible job. I'd like to be your partner in business, Grace Meredith. What do you think about them apples?"

# ChapterThree
# The Partnership

Wonder of wonder, miracle of miracles, Jim and I drew up an uncomplicated plan, easy for me to understand, boundaries clearly defined. Insisting I needed a lawyer, he gave me a list of several in town. Closing my eyes, I picked one. He chuckled, said what a great choice and made the call. Perry Crain arrived within an hour. Meanwhile Jim called a bed and breakfast up the road and booked a room for me. He also called a Doctor Bergen and after a friendly hi and how are you, made an appointment for me to see her tomorrow.

I curled up on a leather couch and watched years drop away from the man I'd met a few hours before. His brown eyes twinkled with energy; every movement he made was like a more youthful man about to begin a journey. Closing my eyes, I dozed to wake when my lawyer, soon to be friend, arrived.

"Sorry to disturb you, Miss Meredith. Jim called and said you needed council. I've been known to lull courtrooms to sleep but not before we've been introduced."

*How adorable*, I thought. *Balding with a white fringe, crinkles around his eyes and mouth from laughter not frowns as far as I could tell through sleepy eyes.* I liked Perry Crain at first glance.

We had the privacy of Jim's office to us while Perry read the agreement and explained it to me before I signed. "This is a fine partnership you've gotten into. Jim doesn't usually trust many people to get close so I'm surprised. You two have been friends along time, I assume."

I smiled thinking if a few hours is a long time, the answer is yes. It's magic. Serendipity. Luck.

"Your fee, Mr. Crain?"

"Jim holds a marker with my name on it. This settles the score. If there's anything I can help you with in the near future, please call. Best wishes in River's Edge, Grace." He handed me a card. "I do have dogs. Two of them. Labradoodles in need of grooming and training. They're young. I realize you won't be set up for business for a while but are you willing to make a house call?"

*Is water wet? Does a bear poop in the woods?* "Since I just got here, my appointment book is almost clear. How about after breakfast tomorrow? I'm staying at the Bed and Breakfast nearby. If someone is home, I can come over and check out your dogs. I love Labradoodles. They're smart."

"Does ten a.m. work for you? My office is at home so I'll be there. Call if there's a problem." We shook hands. Perry Crain left and I twirled around. My first house call! I'll look up the chapter on those curly haired wonder dogs and be ready for them.

"Jim, are you here?"

"Of course. Where else would your new partner be? How did you like my old pal Perry Crain?"

"He's great. You're great." I began to cry. "It's like a dream. Tell me it's really true, Jim."

"Oh, Grace. It's true. I don't know how come you and I met; what set of circumstances set you on this collision course with me but it's real and all good. I'm so grateful. We have an opportunity to bring new life to this beautiful town."

"In more ways than one." I laughed and patted my belly. "Hey, I'm making a house call to Perry Crain's pooches tomorrow. Seems they're out of control and need a bit of Grace training."

He grinned. "By the book?"

"By the biscuit."

# Chapter Four

Waking with a tear soaked pillow case in my new home at Miss Mollie's Bed and Breakfast for the next short time, I sat up disoriented recalling the endless yesterday and all the events that led me to River's Edge. Running away from college and Scott leaving him an incoherent dishonest note. Since when did I lie? Now I'd add that to my sins. No wonder Mother threw me out. And then my luck changed and person by another kind person led me here. I washed the pillow case and myself from top to bottom making a fresh start on this early summer morning. Today I had my first client. Lawyer Perry Crain's puppies and I would get acquainted but first I had to read about the breed and know what to expect.

After breakfast, I thumbed through several of my dog books and found the information needed. Read and reread, make notes was the only way for me to remember so that's what I did.

At ten, heart hammering just like facing a test, I walked down the path to the Crain's door and knocked. A tearful woman opened the door attempting to restrain the puppies.

"Hi, I'm Grace Meredith. I spoke to Mr. Crain last night and he's asked me to see about training your Labradoodles."

She clutched her heart. "Oh thank heavens. They're adorable but out of control. We have no experience with pets and they were supposed to be trained." She gestured to them running around and barking. "I guess the breeder lied."

"Their names?"

"We call them Schnaps and Shtrudle."

"Ah. Do they know their names?"

"Hmm. Come to think of it, no. They just run around and only come to us when food is placed in their bowls."

"Might you and your husband consider giving them simple names? Easy to understand."

"Oh definitely. Anything to make life pleasant. We looked forward to these cuties for a long time and now." She raised her hands palms up as if in frustration.

"Okay. Say the first dog name to come to mind."

She looked at the ceiling, gazed around the room and settled on a card table. "Ace."

"Oh. I like it. And another."

"Deuce."

"You like to play cards." She nodded. "Leave us alone for a while and we'll get to work." An hour later, Mrs. Crain peeked in the room where I literally had Ace and Deuce eating out of my hand. Doodles are an intelligent breed and it didn't take much to train them. They responded well to hand signals and verbal commands rewarded with small biscuits I'd bought at a pet supply shop on Main Street. Not sure as to what I'd charge, I first took the dogs through their paces and had Mrs. Crain follow me a few times. The puppies fell asleep after the workout and many wet smooches. Definitely another shower was needed before the appointment with the obstetrician this afternoon. I loved working with them and when the lady of the house got all weepy and asked me to return for another session to reinforce today's lesson, I agreed. She peeled off fifty dollars and handed it to me. Not knowing what the going rate for a house call was, I thanked her and made a date for the following day.

*Wait 'til Jim hears about this*, I thought. I bought a ledger at the stationery store to keep expenditures and gains for tax purposes. *Grace, you are a woman with a business head. Who'd a thunk it? as they said up in Buffalo.*

With my head held high on a June afternoon when I should have been marching with classmates to graduate from St. Thomas Aquinas University, I began a new life leaving the past behind.

# Chapter Five

Doctor Lorraine Bergen greeted me when I entered a comfortable waiting room for my first appointment. "So you're the young woman Jim called about. He's very impressed with you and warned me to take excellent care or else." Her smile lit up the room filled with wooden toys in one corner, magazines in another, and an array of tea, soda, and a water cooler stand with cups and saucers. Everything one needed to feel at home while waiting. *Cozier than home ever felt to me,* I thought. "Follow me, my dear. Samantha, my nurse called in sick so it's just us chickens today. We'll manage." She flashed another smile. I walked behind her and checked out the graceful way she moved, like a former athlete, posture perfect, and a long gray pony tail bobbed along to her arms swinging back and forth. I felt like a little blob in the wake of a speedboat.

She handed me a gown. "Please remove everything and I can give you a thorough examination."

Left alone, panic set in. So far I hadn't said a word, no papers to fill out, insurance stuff. Jim promised he'd keep my secrets and I believed him.

"Ready or not, here I come."

Still fully dressed, I burst into tears.

"Grace, I'm here to take care of you, be not only your doctor but your friend. Please trust me to do my job. I'm very good. That's why your pal Jim called me. Blink your eyes once for yes if you understand."

I blinked once and giggled and giggled some more.

"That's better. Now let's start fresh. Clothes off." She checked her watch. "I have one hour to be with you. Let's make it a productive one. We'll take care of paper work next visit.

Fast, gentle, efficient. A good description of my new doctor.

"It's no surprise to both of us that you're about three months pregnant. Any nausea, morning sickness?"

"No. Um, Doctor, I ran away from my boyfriend so he doesn't know. We were about to graduate college and we'd known each for a few months so I didn't want to ruin his long term plans and I just left. Without giving him a choice." Afraid to look in her eyes, I chewed on the knuckle of my right thumb.

"Look at me, Grace. Do you really think you're the only girl in the world who faced this decision?" She leaned across the desk saving my thumb. "I did the same thing."

"You did?" Incredulous to learn this educated strong woman was once a kid like me, I almost felt relieved.

"I'm not going into details but I look at you and see me at nineteen and I'm amazed at the similarity between us. So stop biting your thumb. You'll need it for work." She rattled a bunch of notes and shoved them aside. "Ms. Grace Meredith, without checking blood work since Samantha isn't here, I find that you are in spectacular good health. Next visit, in three weeks, we'll continue to monitor you and the baby's progress. Here's a bottle of pre natal vitamins. Take one a day."

"Dr. Feldman gave me a bottle two days ago. He's from a town northwest of here. We met when I was searching for a good safe place to settle."

She jumped out of her chair, ran around the desk and hugged me. "He's a wonderful man. I learned a lot working with him years ago. You keep the vitamins; there's more where that came from, Grace. Now get out and take care." She stopped me with words of caution. "River's Edge is a marvelous place to live in. Beware of gossip and don't take it seriously. Remember we're living in a relatively small town."

"Thanks for everything. I'll call tomorrow for an appointment. See you in three weeks." *Gossip, huh. What did that have to do with me?*

# Chapter Six

Jim and I worked together for part of every day after that first incredible afternoon. The good doctor's words came back to haunt me when I realized the whole town gossiped about the once staid realtor they knew who seemed to be to carrying on with the chick from nowhere.

At the diner one morning, Mimi the owner, walked over to a booth where two women were pointing at me and shaking their heads. In a strong voice, she said, "You don't like our coffee today, ladies?" I didn't know who they were but I knew they had it in for me. The words 'morality' and 'good example' came across loud and clear. Mimi said, "Grace and Jim Trumbull are partners in business at the new Pet Emporium to open real soon" The women snickered. I finished a late breakfast, paid the bill, touched Mimi's shoulder and left. Small towns and gossip. I wasn't prepared for this. As my pregnancy developed, tongues would surely wag at the coffee shop, the bars and every other hang-out for miles around.

Over breakfast at the diner one morning, I saw the same nasty women. Jim greeted them and introduced me. "This is Grace Meredith, my new partner. We're in the midst of rebuilding Dr. Daly's old building into a Dog Grooming business. Grace, this is Dorothy Warren and her sister Laura Warren, President of the Chamber of Commerce." The sisters nodded and murmured hello in unison. *A formidable twosome.* No kindness of strangers here. They stared at my blossoming middle. We walked to our booth dodging bullets or slings and arrows.

"Don't worry about them. They never married and seem to be content with their positions as town gossips. To know you, Grace, is to love you."

*Love me?* I wondered *and dropped the thought like a hot potato. Jim is twenty years older than me. We're just friends or is something more going on?* "Has our partnership hurt your real estate business?"

"If anything, business has improved. My educated guess is folks want to check out the old guy who has a young pregnant girl on the side. They want to be near all the power and hope it rubs off."

We had a good laugh over the image of Super Jim the realtor. I intended to buy him a tee shirt with a big S on the front but somehow the days and nights flew by.

Hungry as always, I hurried to Mimi's Diner for a supplemental breakfast only to regret my decision as soon as the door closed behind me. Loud words spoken by Dorothy Warren carried across for all to hear and aimed at me. "What qualifies you to groom our dogs?"

Thank God for Jim's advice about me getting certified as a Groomer. I enrolled in a certification course by mail the day after I came to town and old study habits kicked in. And I thought college kept me busy. Real life doubled the effort without grades and tests. And now the finished, approved papers were in my backpack and the certificate was at the framers ready to be picked up and hung as soon as the shop, our shop opened.

I kept my cool and smiled to one and all. "I'm a certified Groomer with papers to prove it. If you have pets, know they'll be safe at the Pet Emporium."

Mimi's voice boomed out kitchen doors swinging behind her. "Hey Grace, my bulldog, Roscoe needs an overhaul. Soon as you open, I'll bring him in."

Support from Mimi meant a lot in town. "I make house calls, Mimi. Ask Perry Crain." Waving thanks. I slid into a back booth and ordered chocolate milk and a slice of apple pie. Not quite the diet Dr. Feldman had recommended but sometimes a woman just needed somethin' sweet. A lotta sweet to cover the sour taste left of non-stop gossip. I feared those sisters weren't finished with me and would continue to dig and poke. *Be on your guard, kid,* my inner voice warned. *Be ready to counter-attack at all times. In life there's always the good with the bad.*

I felt a stand-off coming soon at Mimi's Diner. Every time I walked over there, the Warren's came in right after me or were already seated in a booth ready for another confrontation. I didn't intend to cross paths with the likes of them. Conflict. How I disliked it after cowering before my parents all my young life. *No more,* I thought. Too many people thrived on it. This situation required a discussion with my best pal and partner.

On site while carpenters did their thing with our venture into business, Jim and I found boxes to sit on.

"What's up, Grace?"

I sighed. "Gossip is up. The Warren women are using Mimi's Diner to cause trouble and I can't seem to avoid them. So I appeal to you, my friend." *Did I catch a gleam in Jim's eyes when I said those words? Hmm. Be careful of personal involvement. Keep it strictly business.*

He cleared his throat. "They are wicked, those two. Laura Warren won't be able to block your nomination to the Chamber of Commerce. You already have several creditable members who sent letters in recommending you and all you need is two. I counted four and more are forthcoming. But, and here's the big BUTT!"

The last word started laughter as hard as waterfall hitting boulders on the stream. We couldn't stop. The carpenters joined in. They never missed a word despite the hammers and saws making a racket. I wiped tears from my eyes and sipped water to get control.

Jim caught his breath and continued. "They must have a spy."

"A spy?"

"Oh, yes. Someone at the diner is sending a Grace alert when you leave here to walk over there."

"Hmm. It figures. It must be the cashier. She has the best view of the street."

"Right. And I've heard she needs extra cash since her husband is out of work so whatever they're paying her is important."

"How sad, Jim. What can we do? This is real life, not a novel for fun about two spiteful women. Maybe he could work here as a handyman to take up the slack and, and oh, we could ask Mimi to dark curtain one side of the street view so the cashier can't see me until it's too late. Oh, blinds. Wood blinds might work." I thought for another minute or two. "Jim, I need a script, like words to say if I'm confronted again otherwise I'm going to say, "Shut up you nosy bitches and leave me alone."

He appeared to agree and then burst into laughter joined by the workmen."Way to go, Grace. I'll work on it."

Opening day at the Emporium: Special opening day free box of dog biscuits announced in an ad in neighboring newspapers had the phones ringing. I pictured future customers clipping coupons for biscuits if they came in. My assistants and I wore red and blue dog paw print designed smocks. Both Petra and Mike had years of experience, way more than me. I learned from them and I was the boss!

Jim stayed in the background to take notes and say hello if anyone noticed him. "I don't want to steal your thunder, partner. Not on your big day."

Hugging him tight as I could get with my rounder than ever belly in the way, I almost cried. "We've accomplished all this in such a short time, Jim. And you've made me a part of your community. Thank you like, uh forever."

"Forever is good, Grace. My plan is to live a very long life and to be here for your baby to teach her what I know, see her graduate, get married." He smiled. "All the good stuff. Now greet your first customer with a dazzling smile and talk to the dogs in the high pitched voice I've heard you use." It was then

I realized our friendship had grown into a love affair without the sexual undertones. As yet.

"Hi, I'm Grace and these are my trained assistants, Petra and Mike. Welcome to the Pet Emporium." Mike kept the records on the first day; each pet's name, breed and age, owner address, and more while Petra led the dog to a grooming table, talking to the pet in the high voice I'd practiced with my capable assistants. Fur flew, scissors snipped, brushes of different sizes were replaced and cleaned after each pet. Grooming included a wash, ears cleaned and nails clipped. Some customers wanted nail polish on their poodles. Yikes! The day ended with the last bark of approval as I leaned down to whisper in a sad Saluki's ear. She licked my face after a minute or two and perked up when I used long soothing strokes from her sweet head all the way down her back over and over again.

"You whispered to her! Wait until I tell my husband. He wanted to send her back because she just sat around so quiet." Tears filled the woman's eyes." What can I do to help her?"

"Remember she's part of your family. When you take her for a walk, don't talk on the cell phone. Talk to her. Use a higher pitched voice as if she's a baby. Tell her you're proud of her and love her. We're about to close for the night, Mrs." I signaled Mike for a name, "Mrs. Brewster. Bring this precious pooch back to us again and here's a box of nutritious biscuits for a treat."

"Oh I will. Betsy needs obedience training. Do you do that?"

"Yes. We've had great success with some frisky puppies." The doodles came to mind; my first clients.

Doors closed and locked, Mike crunched the numbers and we all did a happy little dance including Jim who turned out to be the best dancer of all. My man of many talents. After splurging on pizza, everyone went home and I had quiet time to go upstairs to my cozy apartment almost finished except for baby furniture. Five months went by and the Pet Emporium business boomed. I didn't fit in our designated smocks

45

anymore and waddled around in a long tee shirt covered by an apron. Some disguise. Everyone knew I was pregnant. Even the dogs. Some serious sniffing went on and they had to be coaxed into the tubs where before most of them couldn't wait to be washed. When Jim didn't have a showing, he spent time at our shop taking over when necessary. While resting my feet up on a chair one afternoon during lunch break, I saw Jim stride in with a Labrador Retriever on a lead.

He bent down and kissed my cheek. "This is Butch. He's a former K-9 dog injured and healed, now retired at way too young so I figured he'd make a good companion for you and the baby. He's just three and needs a good home, Grace." This time he kissed my lips. "We all need a good home."

"Jim, are you proposing something here?"

"I am. I have a large empty home and it needs to be filled with love by you, the baby, Butch, and me. Marry me."

Petra and Mike returned to find us deep in conversation. I told them to take over while Jim and I went for a walk with Butch who limped a tiny bit but seemed strong and obeyed on command. The day had turned cold as winter approached with leaves blowing all over to land in heaps against shop windows. My hood flew back and Jim tied it under my chin. I shivered at his touch. *I did love him for many reasons but marriage? Lose my independence? Maybe a compromise where we might live together in harmony in his comfortable home without vows? Scandalous thought but why not?*

"Let's go to your home and discuss the situation."

Without another word, Jim guided me toward the big Lincoln he drove. In the back I spied a dog bed, kibbles, and a blanket for Butch. The Golden dog hopped right in as if he'd done this for years. "You planned this, you big wonderful man." I kissed him and slid carefully in the passenger seat, mixed thoughts racing around in my muddled mind.

Driving to the residential part of River's Edge, we were quiet, an unusual state for both of us to be in. He pulled into a long driveway, opened a two car garage door, and drove in.

We walked around to the front. "First I'll take Butch for a quick walk," and they disappeared toward a stand of leaf-less trees. I stamped my feet to keep them warm and soon they appeared both looking pleased. Then with a flourish, Jim opened the front door.

"Oh." I gasped at the beauty of the well kept old house, scented with lemon polish, gleaming cherry wood furniture, logs ready to be lit in the huge fireplace. Comfort and beauty combined made my small apartment above the shop seem insignificant by comparison. I pictured the baby growing up here, legitimate with a father who loved her and I almost ran from room to room like a kid touching, embracing everything and finally turned to the one most important person who followed me so patient and quiet.

"Jim. I do care for you and love you and I will marry you right away. And we will raise our little girl in this house as best we can with Butch as her protector and companion. Now show me to the bedroom right now."

# Chapter Seven
# A romance to remember

"It's been a long time for me, Grace. I uh, don't know if I remember how to. . ."

"Oh, hush. You're forty. That's a young man, not even middle age." I helped him undo the buttons of his shirt and didn't care if his muscles didn't ripple like an athlete. Knowing his feelings for me, how he'd taken me under his capable arms and made me his partner the first time we met; that's what counted. We were a perfect fit despite a twenty years difference. I'd been old since growing up in my parent's stultified atmosphere where childhood meant nothing.

"Honey, I don't have much experience either so let's wing it and do what comes naturally."

After a tentative beginning, Jim and I found each other and did the dance of love, careful not to disturb the baby inside. The sweetness of it all being wrapped in the arms of my lover and soon-to-be husband. Fragrant wisteria scented lotion, my favorite, poured first to warm in his big hands and gently Jim spread it over my body beginning with my shoulders and moving down. Between my fingers and over the swelling where he smiled as the baby gave a kick and roll. My breasts were more than a handful now and he paused to admire them rubbing a bit of lotion then tasting everywhere. Pausing lower, I urged him to go on lifting my hips feeling heat inside and when his erection pressed against my thigh, reached for it marveling at the size.

"Oh, Jim. You are one hunk of a man. My man." Almost incoherent with desire, I moved him in place and felt skin against skin for the first time without the barrier of protection.

"Deeper, deeper, sweetheart." He filled me completely and made me want to sing at the top of my voice but I knew the spell might break so I gasped and loved every moment. When release came and it did for both of us, we curled up in a comfy spoon position and napped to wake later with a bark from the latest member of the family. Butch needed attention.

Jim grabbed his robe, a big blue terry cloth one in need of repair or the Goodwill basket, and stumbled downstairs after our dog. *Our dog,* I thought. *Our home, our baby, our new life. All good.* A fleeting thought of Scott Dwyer passed through my mind. He must be in school somewhere, arms around some campus cutie. My one and only love no more, replaced by a fine man. I prayed Jim and I had many good healthy years ahead of us to raise precious Cindy and give her the love I never had except for once in a while from my dear grandfather.

After the necessary documents were filled out, Jim and I were married at the Justice of the Peace in town witnessed by our lawyer Perry Crain and his wife Crystal. We celebrated at River's Edge Finest, inside this time. The bride, that's me, wore a white lace tent and white new sneakers. Laughter as we toasted. They drank champagne. I had white grape juice. Larry Owens stopped by to join us and picked up the tab. "I would have been flower girl or ring bearer if you'd called. Oh well. The christening is on you." More laughter. A few kicks and rolls from inside and I settled down to eat slowly and enjoy our wedding dinner.

After closing one evening, I climbed up on a ladder to straighten the star at the top of the Christmas tree. I remember watching snow fall thick and heavy enough to cover bushes on the walkway just before water flowed between my legs. Jim had warned me not to climb or do anything strenuous. Stubborn as always, I chose to do it my way.

"Help. My water broke. Someone call Jim. Call Dr. Bergen." No one answered. I forgot the staff had gone home. Alone I hung on tight to the ladder careful not to fall and reached the floor to walk through the puddle and call Jim.

"Help. It's time, Jim. Should I call the police?"

"I'll take care of you, dear Grace. Hang on and breathe just as we practiced."

My good doctor and friend after what seemed like endless months of pregnancy, Lorraine Bergen, stayed at my side through ten hours of labor and delivered our red faced beautiful baby.

Cindy Scooter Trumbull gave a war cry as she entered this world and hasn't stopped since that epic moment. James Trumbull became daddy to his sweet girl and taught her with wisdom and kindness all the days of his life.

I remembered kind Dr. Feldman and located the business card he'd given me on that fateful day. All he asked for in return was a holiday hello every year.. I scribbled a note about the good luck I'd found in River's Edge and my new partner in business and marriage and our baby girl. This became a tradition for a long time until one year my Christmas greeting was returned. Sadness filled my heart. A connection broken.

# Chapter Eight
## One day at a time

"Once upon a time," Jim rocked our three month old baby as he read a bed time story. Every night we hoped for a peaceful night's sleep. Her blue eyes closed and he kept rocking for a while longer. His eyes closed too and his head slumped forward. I lifted pink bundled Cindy from him and propped her on her side in the nursery next door to our room. Butch padded in after me, circled three times in his dog bed and settled down to guard his small charge. Now to rouse Jim and put him to bed; a mother's work is never done.

"Honey, time to go to sleep. Quick before she wakes up. Again. Maybe this night she'll sleep right through."

"Right through 'til two in the morning. My time to feed her then or yours. I forgot."

"Mine." I dived under the covers and passed out. No time for romance or a kiss goodnight.

We marked the calendar the next morning, astonished after a double take at the clock. Our precious girl had slept from ten at night 'til six in the morning. A milestone. She sapped all our energy for the time being and now, as the saying goes, we could see a glimmer at the end of the tunnel.

I didn't trust anyone yet to care for her so off we went each morning, baby needs packed in a carrier, and I worked. Petra and Mike always helped out but the Pet Emporium had grown in six months and the possibilities seemed endless.

Mimi from the diner hurried over one morning, a woman in tow behind her. "Grace, this is Rachel Brown. She's a baby nurse, just retired from St. Paul's Hospital three towns south of here and she wants to continue working."

After thanking Mimi and promising her a zillion free sessions with Roscoe, her bulldog, my attention turned to Mrs. Brown.

Love at first sight. One look at the white haired woman with the kind pale blue eyes and I felt a kinship. Somewhere in my woe be gone background, Mother must have hired a pleasant woman to take care of me for a while and here she was, reincarnated to help raise Cindy. I showed her around the shop and the apartment upstairs, introduced her to Butch and finally he allowed her near the baby.

"I want Jim, my husband, to meet you, Mrs. Brown."

"Call me Rachel and you are?"

"Oh, uh, I'm so excited. I'm Grace. Grace Trumbull. Do you have a place to live? We have a large house. Comfortable, lots of room and well, you'll see that is if you'll take the job and live with us like forever."

Rachel laughed. "You'll want to check my credentials and give me a trial run."

"I will? Oh yes, of course, I will. Get Jim on the phone someone, please."

And after Jim walked over to see what the fuss was all about, we sat down like grown-ups and struck a deal. Life settled down after dear funny Rachel joined the family. She became like a wondrous character in one of my favorite stories from childhood; the story of Mary Poppins, a British series about a special kind of nanny.

# Chapter Nine
## Cindy's questions

Content to play with toys and all of us at home, once Cindy started pre-school at three she returned asking questions. "How come I don't have cousins like Susie?" Or "How come I don't have a baby brother, sister, auntie, uncle, grandma's and grandpa's?" She missed relatives no matter that she had a loving daddy, mommy, Rachel, and Butch. She wanted more. I knew the feeling to some degree. Jim and I discussed it with me pacing the floor wringing my hands feeling inadequate again.

The voice of reason prevailed when he said, "She's acting out. In truth, Cindy has more than enough so don't worry. We're not going to adopt a child and we agreed one is enough with both of us in business."

One day when she was four, she came home with the last straw that literally cracked my sense of sanity.

"Mommy, what's illa, um, I can't remember the bad word Lena called me."

Tears rolled down her smooth rosy cheeks and broke my heart. My past had caught up with me. Someone at pre-school said she was illegitimate. Gossip begun when I moved to River's Edge rose up to hurt my child. My hope that by marrying Jim before she was born, Jim legally became her father and Cindy would be protected from stigma. But no. Small town gossip never died. It smoldered for a while and erupted years later. My inner lioness roared and reawakened to protect my cub.

Drying her tears, I offered a chocolate chip cookie. Lower lip trembling she turned it down and climbed on my lap, her legs dangled, baby fat long gone. *She looked just like Scott,* I thought, *with his blue eyes, curly blond hair and athlete's build.* "Do you know Lena's last name?"

"Lena Warren. Dummy, stupid Lena, Meana. Call her mommy and tell her not to say that word or I'll." She made two small fists and punched the air.

"Rachel needs you to help walk Butch now, honey. I'll call the school and get Lena's phone number." She grabbed the cookie and ran through the house, Butch at her heels calling for her pal, the baby nurse who came and stayed to join our little family. Of course I called Jim. I felt his outrage at the insult to our child through the phone.

"Lena Warren is the kid's name. She must be related in some way to those sisters who tried to make life miserable for me five years ago. A cousin's child or distant relative since they were spinsters, old maids, bitches."

"Damn those women. I'll do an immediate check on who the relative is and get a number. This must be stopped before it goes any further. Grace, don't jump the gun. Let me get the information and we'll write a script just as we've done before. Many times. We want this to be a bloodless coup."

I laughed. Better than crying. Ever since he figured out those women paid someone to spy on me about five years ago, Jim loved to play detective.

With nothing to do for a few minutes, I paced the kitchen, opened and closed a lot of cabinets and found a box of Mac and Cheese. Water boiled just like the blood boiling inside me. No simmering for me when I thought way back to the short time when I never said no to Scott Dwyer. On the other hand, I wouldn't have this beautiful daughter and my darling Jim and my whole life changed all because I never said no.

I stirred and waited for noodles to cook and the phone to ring. I read the box as if it were news to me. At least four times a week the preferred meal for my kid. Cut the packet and pour in the cheese. *What a cook.* The phone rang. A quick cover jammed on the pot and I picked up on the second ring.

"Okay, Grace. Sit down but first turn off the burner."

"How did you know? Am I so predictable?"

"Not you. Our daughter is. Mac and Cheese, right?"

We shared a laugh and his tone grew serious. "It seems long ago Dorothy Warren married for a short time and her husband, an unsavory guy with jail time needed to escape from her so they divorced while she was pregnant."

"Hmm. Secrets unveiled."

"More. Much more. She gave the baby up for adoption but when a distant relative, you were so right, heard about said baby, he and his wife adopted the child, a boy. There's the connection. Now Mark Warren, adopted child all grown-up has a little girl named Lena."

"Who goes to pre-school with Cindy. Jim, how do we nip this before it spreads? My impulse is to go to the source, Dorothy, and tell her we know about her baby, gossip etc and."

"Or go to Mark Warner, tell him we know about his past and we insist he stop his kid from maligning our child. Hmm. He may not know he's adopted. Let's do it your way. I'll get the less than Honorable Miss Warren to come to my office for a little chat. Join us at," she heard him sifting through papers, "four today."

"How do you know she'll be available, Jim?"

"The Shadow Do." And he did an impersonation of a spooky laugh from a long ago radio program he'd told her about.

She hung up laughing. Cindy, Rachel and Butch transformed the house when they stomped in, cheeks rosy from an outside romp and tail wagging, the Golden Labrador Retriever had a goofy smile on his long doggy face.

They washed their hands and sat for a sumptuous feast, their faithful companion's background chomp and slurp to accompany the meal.

I hurried up to check on a decent wardrobe for the occasion. No more the pregnant kid from nowhere, Grace Trumbull was the impressive owner of the Pet Emporium and wife of the prominent realtor in River's Edge, James Trumbull. The soft grey wool suit would do. Short jacket with a little flare below the waist and a skirt that hung in a few unpressed pleats. Just right for me said the New York City saleswoman at Bergdorf Goodman Jim insisted we go to. Forehead bangs changed my straight brown hair to a new look. Silver hoop earrings gave the finishing touch and by four I sat in Jim's inner office, legs crossed, waiting for Dorothy Warren.

The voice pierced the air before she barreled in. My insides quivered. "What's this all about, Jim? What could be so important you had to drag me away from my knitting circle this afternoon."

"Calm down, Dorothy. We have a major problem to discuss with you."

"We? Who's we?" And then she saw me at the conference table, sipping hot tea in an attempt to appear in charge.

"You know my wife, Grace."

"Yes." She spun around. "I need coffee, lots of sugar."

Jim poured a fresh mug full of what she requested. A plate of cookies were on the table. Like a greedy child, she grabbed two.

We sat in silence while Dorothy settled in. Then Jim began. He started with the name calling at pre-school and the offender's name, Lena Warren caused her eyes to widen. "The name Warren reminded me of you so I did a bit of backtracking and found that you're related to this child. Our daughter is not illegitimate. I am Cindy's father." I.Do.Not.Want.Our.Child.To.Suffer.From.Gossip." He gave her a wicked smile. "Do you understand, Dorothy?"

"No. What the hell are you talking about?" She stood so quickly, coffee spilled all over the front of her skirt. Jim slid napkins across the table and gestured for her to sit. She did.

"We know about your marriage to a man with a jail record and then your subsequent divorce, giving your baby away for adoption to a relative." Her face turned pale. "There are no secrets, Dorothy and gossip is mean. We can spread this news, true news not made up the way you smeared Grace when she first moved here. We can and will if you don't go to Mark Warren and his wife to tell them their little four year old daughter Lena has started to slander our Cindy. She heard the word illegitimate somewhere and my educated guess is it came from you."

She cried. "I want my sister and I want her now."

Jim and I exchanged glances and shrugged. "Call her if you must. It won't change any thing. This is up to you, Dorothy so fix it. That's your specialty. Grace and I will keep your secrets. But I warn you," Jim stood and towered over the woman who had caused me so much grief. "if we ever hear one mean word about our child's heritage, we'll go after you."

Still sobbing, Dorothy Warren grabbed a few more cookies and her handbag and slammed the door.

We sat silent for a while. "You're scary when someone crosses you, Jim."

"That's how I sell more real estate than anyone for miles around. Now get over here and sit on my lap."

# Chapter Ten

The first stroke happened when Jim and I were walking with Butch through the snow one night. My husband stumbled. The cold wind blew snow around and I reached up to make sure Jim's scarf still covered his neck when I found him staring at nothing, one side of his mouth sagging. *Oh God, please no.* "Jimmy, talk to me, sweetheart." He turned his head and mumbled incoherently. Slowly I guided him back to the house and called for Rachel who came running down the stairs. "Help me. Help us."

"What's going on, Grace?" One look at my husband and she said, "I think he's had a TIA. I've seen this before."

Removing Jim's outerwear, Rachel led him to the living room to lie down. Unsteadily using Rachel's support, he somehow got to the couch and collapsed. With her expertise, she arranged him in a more comfortable position and turned to me after I called Andrew Blake, our family doctor and good friend.

"What's a TIA?"

"Transient Ischemic Attack. Minor stroke. Is Doctor Blake coming right away? Otherwise we'll call 911."

The doorbell rang. Andrew Blake must have used his son's cop car with flashing lights. "Andy, Jim's in here."

Wrapped in a warm blanket on the couch lay my bewildered husband lost in a fog we couldn't penetrate. I hovered nearby while Andy performed his magic and finally nodded saying the same words Rachel said a short while before. "Jim's had a TIA. There must be a blood clot that broke loose slowing the blood flow to his brain temporarily. It's essential for him to be seen by a top neurologist right away. I'll make a call and get someone to examine him tonight. The best and closest care right now is nearby St. Paul's in Lincolnshire about twenty miles south. An ambulance is on the way. This is a crucial time after TIA's to hopefully prevent further strokes."

He paused, exchanging a worried glance with me. *My darling in danger. Out of nowhere, walking in the snow on a winter night, life reminds you how fragile you are. A grain of sand on the beach of life.*

"Yes, I'll pack a" The siren of an ambulance split the air.

"No need to pack now. The hospital has everything Jim needs for tonight. Follow us there."

"I'm going with Jim."

"You'll be in the way, Grace. Get in your car and drive carefully. Rachel, you'll keep the home fires burning and don't worry Cindy. Jim's going to be all right."

After kissing Jim and assuring him I'd be at his side soon, I watched my precious husband being lifted onto a stretcher and out the door in falling snow. Always on top of everything, Rachel handed me a bag she'd packed with amenities if I stayed overnight. "I'll call when I know something more. When Cindy comes home tell her. . ."

"I'll figure out something close to the truth, Grace. Tell the good folks at St. Paul's I'm a member of your family. They'll take extra good care of our Jim."

The words further strokes repeated in the whirl of my mind spinning round and round all the way to the hospital.

An MRI showed a clot in the carotid artery dangerous enough to cause a more serious stroke. Dr. Bernstein, a well known neurosurgeon, friend of Andy Blake spoke freely to Jim and me after another of a series of examinations. "Your brain has to cool for thirty days before I can operate."

I winced hearing about Jim's brain having to cool.. It sounded so science fiction. "Meanwhile don't do anything strenuous like shoveling the driveway. Gentle sex is all right." Jim flushed red in the cheeks and I thought, *Yay! Better than nothing.* "You're a young man." He looked at his chart. "Forty nine. I predict a long life ahead for you after this problem is resolved."

We made an appointment for the surgery in spring and pale faced I drove home, Jim beside me, thoughtful his mind clear.

"This is a big deal operation, Grace. I'll have a dueling scar down the side of my neck."

"Dueling? You don't know how to fence, silly."

"I mean it. Will you still love me with a scarred neck? Tell me the truth."

I pulled over into a small deserted park and showed him how much I loved him. When I finished and said, "There's more of that after the surgery, big boy," we continued traveling the familiar two lane road and reached our home. Cindy and Rachel had hung a long banner of Welcome Home, Daddy from all of us with hearts and flowers decorations. Somehow time had passed since the wintery night of the TIA and Valentine's Day approached. I shook my head in disbelief. Petra and Mike held down the fort at our Pet Emporium and Trumbull Realtor still rated number 1 in sales thanks to the faithful staff and good will of customers.

Jim, a grateful smile on his face, hugged Cindy. "How's school, my girl? Tell me all about your friends, teachers, homework and just plain stuff."

"Dad, you're so much better. I can tell. First, I have a boyfriend. I didn't tell you when you were sick but now I can, right?"

I waved to Jim over Cindy's head and mouthed okay with a thumbs up.

"Well sure. What's his name and does he like sports?"

Cindy's words spilled over to an interested father and I left the two of them to see what smelled so good in the kitchen. From now on we'd be on low fat or no-fat, fruit and vegetable, chicken and fish diet. *Hmm. Sounded like my pregnancy routine. And no chocolate for nine months. What a pain!*

Rachel pulled out the broiler tray with seasoned golden chicken filets and little red potatoes ready to eat. Steamed broccoli with a pat of better than butter, *oh really?* melting on top heaped high in a white tray. She rang the dinner bell.

"What's the good word, Grace?"

"Carotid artery surgery in a month."

"Well, we'll deal with that one day at a time."

And for the first time since that dreadful scary night, we all sat down for dinner together.

# Chapter Eleven

"The surgery went well." the nurse said. "I'll bring you in soon to see your husband."

I paced the floor, waited and paced some more. Alone by choice, I had a book to read and never read. Two hours went by. *Soon, she said. Two hours is way longer than soon.* I cursed under my breath as relatives came and went everyone happy except for me. I called for a nurse, a someone in charge demanding to know what was going on.

"Mrs. Trumbull." I jumped up to face a starched older nurse. "There's been a complication with your husband."

"Complication?"

The operation went well but in the recovery room his blood pressure went high and then plummeted very low. Doctor Bernstein put in an emergency pacemaker to regulate his heart beat and now it's stable." She caught me as I slipped to the floor. *Too much tension.* She called for a glass of water. I sipped and recovered.

"He's all right? He's not going to die?"

"He's all right. You can see him right now. Please don't alarm him. You've both had enough trauma for one day."

She took my wrist and checked my pulse. My heart pounded. *Slow down. Be strong. I can't. Yes, I can.* "He's my rock."

Her kind eyes gazed into mine as if she saw the life I'd lived before I met Jim. "Now you be his."

Operations can change a person, especially anything to do with the heart and brain. Jim just had both and now he worried and waited for the other shoe to drop. I noticed his confidence wane as he spoke slower, softer, afraid of the effort to strain himself. Cindy was the only one he felt comfortable enough to be the old before-he-got-sick Daddy Jim. I became the cheerleader in the house, bouncing around like everything was cool. Finally I ran out of steam and brought a puppy home. Just what we needed to boost spirits, this three month old white with brown whiskers Wirehaired Pointer worked his way into our hearts the first day. Jim came out of his shell to begin life with a fresh attitude.

Butch tolerated the pup we named Boomer because he launched himself from one place to another and wore himself out to snuggle beside our old dog. No need to buy another bed for Boomer. He slept curled next to his furry master until sadly Butch departed a few years later.

Every month Jim had a date by phone with someone who called to check his pacemaker and make sure it still worked well. The phone rang right on time. He'd pick it up to verify his name and number and place the phone against the place on his chest where the pacemaker was implanted. He'd hang up, grin with a thumbs up and we'd breathe sighs of relief. Except for my husband's regimen of pills three times a day, mild exercise and a healthy diet, our little family adjusted well.

Until hippies came to town. On the outskirts of town, a group of young men and women formed some kind of commune. They dressed in torn jeans and loose gauze shirts made in India, I thought, after seeing one close up. The women were bra-less, said oh wow a lot, wore flowers in their hair and the guys wore head bands and earrings with feather or gold studs. They opened a run-down shop at the end of Main Street and sold their wares.

Parents were called to the high school for counseling about drugs. Drugs? In River's Edge? Watch out for strangers hanging around the school peddling marijuana, we were warned. JUST SAY NO posters hung from every lamppost. I read a book written by Peter Benchley titled Jaws and all I could think of is "just when you thought it was safe to go into the water." Kids wanted to try something new, something parents objected to. Our Cindy, busy with gymnastics and piano lessons, never mentioned drugs. I wondered if I should bring it up or wait and see. And then the worst happened. Cindy's close friend, Amanda Cummings who suffered from asthma tried marijuana, choked and died before help came.

Sadness enveloped our town. Hippies disappeared in a cloud of smoke never to be seen again. We were scarred from the loss of one of our own. Both kids and parents grieved and eventually flowers bloomed, snow fell, seasons changed and we survived. I never had the talk about drugs with my daughter. Never had to. When graduation came, a space was left to honor the memory of Amanda Cummings.

Our daughter went on to graduate college and Law School.

Jim reached out and touched my hip one night. A tentative loving flow of heat went from his hand to my body. In the quiet of our home, we could carry on like wild lovers but that time had passed with his illness taking a toll. Heart medications changed a person. Our romantic love slowed to a crawl. I longed for more and settled for less because we cared for each other.

"Grace?"

"I'm here."

"I love you."

"Prove it, big boy." Soon we were a tangle of bed clothes and sheets like in the old days. I kissed his mouth, cheeks, neck, to work my way down to the pacemaker where I planted soft kisses. "You like?"

"I like."

A few swirls of my tongue on his nipples got me all hot and bothered. "Your turn."

He moaned. "Do I have to?"

"Yes. It's your punishment."

We had fun that night and many more nights before his heart gave out.

The last words my darling said to me were, "I love you." The next morning I woke up. Jim didn't.

The word funeral drummed in my ears. Frantic phone calls, Cindy rushing home from New York with her fiancée, Len. Arrangements to make. Rachel took over with catering for a wake. Open or closed casket? Open at peace with favorite pictures tucked around my beloved. Buster's old ball thrown many times also placed among his favorite things to take on his next journey. And cremation as we'd decided, ashes to be strewn in the stream below the falls beyond River's Edge in a private ceremony with Cindy.

Following a trail to the stream about five miles north of town, Cindy led the way carrying the urn with Jim's ashes with me clinging to every branch in fear of falling. We looked at each other, at the urn and at the stream filled with rushing water over rocks large and small. "It's time, Mom." She opened the top and together we poured what was left of our sweet man in a place he loved. "He's in heaven, Mom. Above and now right here." She touched her heart. We didn't cry. So many tears had been shed since he left us. I felt hollow inside. My partner in business and life was gone. Nothing left for me to do. Excitement and challenge each day brought because of our teamwork had ended. I looked at a blank slate and didn't know how to fill it.

Showing homes to prospective buyer's needed an experienced person so I appointed Jim's long time associate, Claudia Wilcox, the manager of Trumbull Realtor. Caressing every piece of furniture he ever touched in our home became a habit. Both tears and fingerprints left a trail. One day Rachel sat me down in the kitchen.

"Grace, the furniture is cleaned with lemon polish and it's high time you stopped leaving your mark on everything. I'm too old to be wiping up after you, dear girl." She lifted my chin. "You're wasting away to nothing and we both know Jim wouldn't want you to grieve your big heart out. Either go to counseling or get your ass back to work hard and you'll be better."

"Ass?"

"You heard me, young lady."

Time to pull my act together. Someone once said if you act happy and stay busy, soon you'll be happy and successful. I gave it a shot.

The Pet Emporium needed an extension to accommodate demands from customers. Jim had taken photos of the old building and the restoration when we formed our partnership. I loved the sound of hammers and saws, give and take of the crew as they worked a magical transformation. When the carpenters finished the big project, I had a photographer combine the three stages of growth representing our dream. On a glorious spring day my staff and I had an open house to honor our customers.

First we had the two red fire engines at the head of a parade followed by a float with our dog clients, big and small, all dependable obedience trained. Experienced handlers from all over requested a chance to be part of the day and after vetting them, no one was turned down. The high school marching band came next in full blue and white regalia, baton twirlers, cheerleaders and acrobats in order. New York City papers covered the story as well as local news.

I recalled our opening years before with me at nineteen, pregnant giving away a box of dog treats with a coupon for each appointment. Jim in the background, smiling his approval.

This time we gave dog tags away with each appointment. A stamping machine paid for itself in one day. A light buffet catered by Mimi's Diner and watched over by her number one and two waiters kept the place hopping. Petra and Mike, my faithful groomers for years need more help and I'd hired two more young people with experience and a bookkeeper/receptionist to keep track of business. As for me, I smiled a lot, greeted new and old customers like nothing had changed. Deep inside, I changed. For better, in spite of myself.

# Chapter Twelve
## I'm Fifty Four. How did that happen?

"Mother, when did your menopause end?"

Warning bells sounded in my head when daughter, Cindy called me Mother. She turned a two syllable word into three with accent on the first. "Honey, that's an odd question to ask but the answer is I haven't started menopause."

"You mean you still get your uh, cycle?"

"Well, if you really must know, yes. I'm only fifty four and."

"Meet us at River's Edge Steak House in half an hour."

*Bossy only child*, I thought and hurried to change from my working smock as owner of the Pet Grooming Emporium on Main Street in upstate New York, to wear something more appropriate to the fanciest restaurant for miles around. Fortunately Cats day finished early, my end of the day assistant Kathy had swept the floors clean and left.

Alone, I surveyed the few outfits hanging in the closet and wrinkled my nose. Time to lose ten or twenty pounds and buy fresh, more up-to-date clothes. *For what? For yourself, you dope. Take pride in all you've accomplished. Oh yeah. The me I've forgotten about.*

Showered and dressed in a loose blue sweater and long flowered skirt, I looked in the full length mirror. What stared back was an aging hippie sans beads and flowers in my hair. Searching through my jewelry box, I found the gold locket on a thin chain given to me by my first love. College--1960. I hooked the gold chain around my neck.

I drove the fifteen miles through sleepy rush hour traffic in River's Edge, waving to customers if they honked or yelled, "Hey." Small towns where life is simple. My daughter lives further south closer to New York City where she and her husband, Len, commute to work each day. Both lawyers, childless after years of fertility treatments. Hmm. Can this sudden interest in my menopause be linked to the personal question about me?

I pulled into the parking lot of the rustic lodge to be greeted by the owner himself, Larry Owens and his current hunting dog, Buddy Boy, a Golden Retriever I groomed often. I had a fleeting thought about the time Larry asked if I'd uh, consider grooming him once in a while. We remained friends because I didn't smack the married man upside his attractive head. I'd never forget the evening when I'd stumbled into River's Edge, met my best new friend, married that wonderful man, Jim Trumbull, who introduced me to Larry. And now sadly, my precious Jim had passed on after guiding me through years of love, business and the wonder of motherhood.

A handsome devil, actually the master and his dog, one kissed my chubby cheek, the other slobbered lavish wetness on my open palm. Nice to be welcomed on a summer night after all the meowing through the day.

"Cindy and Len are waiting for you. We seated them outside with a terrific view of the falls and the river."

"Thanks, Larry. I know the way."

He took my arm anyway and escorted me up the old wooden steps, through the beamed ceiling rooms and gleaming planked walls through the glass doors at the rear. I heard the rush of water hitting rocks on the plunge down the mountain and falling into the river bed before I recognized Cindy's voice.

"Mother, we're here." Len stood and pulled back a chair for me to sit at a cozy round table for three.

A shrimp cocktail, my favorite, waited for me with a small silver two pronged fork and two lemon slices. Also a crystal glass of Chardonnay sat begging my lips to take a sip. I had a distinct feeling this pre-order was a haste not to waste a moment of precious time.

*Am I this predictable,* I wondered recalling Jim saying that to me during a moment of romance. *Like same old Mom.* "What's the rush, kids? Maybe I choose not to have shrimp cocktail tonight."

"Oh, Mom, you always, always begin with this appetizer. Right, Len?"

He nodded and lifted his wine glass. "A toast to the three of us." And for some reason soon to become apparent to me, Len cleared his throat. "As you know, we've been going through fertility treatments for five years now and finally Dr. Ingersol suggested we either consider adoption or."

Cindy cut in. "He also suggested surrogacy and I," she cast a steady look at her husband, "we want to ask you, because we trust you, dear Mom, to be our surrogate."

I choked on a shrimp and gulped down the Chardonnay. "Surrogate as in having your baby?" Was the pounding I heard the sound of the nearby falls or an imminent heart attack? "Do I have to uh, sleep with Len?"

They laughed. I held my breath. "No. It's done by insemination. Dr. Ingersol will explain everything. And I have two frozen eggs we'll use in addition to um, well. Just say yes and it will work out."

Their eager young faces looked at me, the dependable mom who never said no. Automatically I touched the gold locket. I never said no to him either and here I sat some thirty plus years later with our daughter asking please. Big sacrifice for me to possibly carry a baby so my daughter would have a child of her own. Could I do it? Yes. For her, anything. Would I do it was another question.

"You realize this comes as a huge surprise. I'll have to think it over and get back to you Let's have dinner and Cindy, you can tell me about such a procedure step by step since you've been living with infertility issues for several years." I focused my attention on the dearest son-in-law I ever hoped to have. "Len, do you have any calls to make or shows you might watch while we talk?"

"Sure, Mom. A bit of both. It's been a long day. For all of us."

# Chapter Thirteen

Len settled down in Jim's home office while Cindy and I sat on the new leather couch purchased recently.

She ran her hands over the buttery yellow soft material. "Nice. I thought you might sell the old house."

I shivered at the thought. "And leave my golden memories behind? No. I feel Jim is here and my pooches keep me company." The rapid click of paws in the hall alerted me to company coming. Princess and Prince wagged short tails in greeting. My sweet miniature poodles followed commands before I allowed them up on our laps.

Cindy ran her hand through Prince's curly hair and scratched behind his ears. "They almost match the couch."

Their apricot color complemented the yellow tone and I had added decorative cushions in brown, yellow and an orange shade. *What a decorator. I couldn't dress myself but oh baby, just give me paint and pillows and dogs.* "Do you like it?"

"Very much. Now let's get down to business."

I glanced at my daughter. While she appeared calm, I detected hurt in her eyes. I'd held her hand through despair that she wasn't successful in conceiving; a major failure after reaching success in the highly competitive world of lawyers. In my mother's heart I wanted to heal her and give her the baby she coveted if at all possible. Len had gone with her to all the prior fertility treatments and now it was my turn to step up to the plate.

"I've made a chart of what you can expect step by step. It's a tedious process so don't be discouraged. Are you ready, Mom?"

Almost saluting my bossy precise daughter, I said, "Yes, I am."

"Step One. You must meet with a psychologist but with your background, I'm sure you'll pass the test."

I laughed. "Thanks for the faith in little old mom."

"You're not old. Don't say that three letter word again. Step Two. Here's a tricky part. To coordinate our menstrual cycles we'll take birth control pills."

I laughed and couldn't stop at the thought of birth control pills. If only I'd taken them, remembered to take them thirty five years ago, we wouldn't be having this conversation tonight. I clutched her hand and finally caught my breath.

"What's so funny?"

"Oh baby girl. The words birth control cracked me up. Continue please and don't pay attention if I seem like I'm off my rocker every once in a while." *I wondered if Jim listened in from heaven and enjoyed a hearty laugh.*

"Dr. Ingersol will give you a physical examination. Also an ultrasound and disease screening. an overall health screening. Don't panic, Mom. You'll like the nice doctor."

"Oh my God, Cindy, you sound just like I did when I'd take you to a doctor. "You'll like the nice doctor and then if you're a good girl you'll get a lollipop." This time we both giggled.

"Honey, I hate the sound of this but it's okay. I'm in."

She breathed what sounded like a sigh of relief and consulted her notes.

"Oh, the first day of menstrual cycle and then you begin an evaluation cycle that takes about three weeks."

"Hmm."

"Then, and here comes the big one, we both take birth control pills to coordinate cycles and then a sonogram on you, legal contract signed, Pap smear, treatment cycle and medication to keep from ovulating to receive embryo and," she read faster and faster like a train going downhill. "I take meds to stimulate follicles to release eggs. Three days after eggs are retrieved and fertilized, embryo is transferred to Surrogate. Eleven days later Surrogate is checked for pregnancy. If positive," tears streaked her lovely face smearing eye make-up but who cared, "an ultrasound may be done to determine the sight of implantation and often a heartbeat." We cried together. She finished with the final words, "At four weeks a positive fetal heartbeat may be heard if all goes well."

"How about a glass of wine and some chocolate covered strawberries before our lives are turned upside down?"

"I'll drink to that." Len strolled into the living room and sat down. The dogs jumped into his waiting arms. "We must head home soon, Mom. You girls have a fun time?" He brought a box of tissues from the kitchen and handed it over.

After they left, I walked my little pals to the backyard for a final chance to mark their territory and we all headed upstairs, the house quiet. I decided to roll with the program and not worry what came next. My fate was sealed the moment I'd agreed to be surrogate for them. *Sorry? Maybe. In truth, hell yes. So be it. At last I'd give my daughter what she wanted more than anything else in the world.*

Rubbing his hands together as if he anticipated the beginning of a great event, Dr. George Ingersol gave me, his new patient, the once over twice. "Welcome Grace Trumbull. I've heard about you for years, way before Cindy became my patient, regarding the Pet Emporium. You are called the dog whisperer."

*An aw shucks moment.* I managed a smile. "Over rated, Doctor." Gazing at the sci-fi appearance of his office, I recalled Rod Serling's long ago Twilight Zone series on early television. His words, "Being like everybody is the same as being nobody," came back to me. Being a surrogate at my age lifted me out of the everybody class according to the brilliant writer. I like that.

"You've passed the psychologist's examination and today we'll get serious."

*Serious? I thought we'd passed serious when I agreed to come here.* "Mrs. Wilcox will attend to you before the physical." The trim woman in white took over by handing me a gown. I knew the drill. I'd showered all my parts and dropped my drawers on a neat shelf, folding and hanging as need and steeped out of the private cubicle. Lights, camera, action. Dr. Ingersol returned, armed with enough of an arsenal to explore King Tut's tomb in fantasy land. Eyes shut tight, I prayed for the torture to be over, pass the exam and move to the next phase of what? Oh yes, a sonogram thingy and health inspection. What in the world have I gotten myself into for the sake of my kid and her kid. I focused on petulant poodles, crying Chihuahua's, adorable doodles, sad Salukis and after an interminable time the ordeal ended.

Rubber gloves snapped off, lights turned on and the nice doctor helped me sit. "This is looking very promising, Grace. Schedule another appointment at the front desk."

"I will, George." After all, the nice doctor had just gone where no man had ventured since my sweetheart died. And he didn't take me out for dinner, no drinks, nothing not even a kiss. And now he wanted me to return on command.

He shot me a look, tilted his head and grinned. *He got the irony*, I thought.

"Please leave a business card at the desk. I have a serious Schnauzer who needs lightning up."

On the way home, I thought about Doctors and patients. They call us by our first names and we're expected to use a title to address them. I studied hard to get be a Certified Pet Groomer. Plus I'm in my mid fifties. I command respect for all my work. So what if I gave up dreams of becoming a veterinarian because I never said no. And my obstetrician, Lorraine Bergen and I became good buddies when I was nineteen and she was forty. So there.

# Chapter Fourteen

*Three months later*

After a dinner filled with joyful tears and lots of glance at my middle making me squirm until I had to say, "Stop," Len asked for privacy to catch up on some calls and we drove back to my home. Cindy squeezed my hand.

"We have a bit of catching up to do, Mom."

Sleep following a busy day of grooming and dinner, I wanted to rest my weary head. "Catching up about what, honey.? So far we're on a successful path with the baby, I'm following doc's orders. So what's to catch up?"

Len parked and in we went to my big old home where Cindy grew up. "Use my office, Len. Mi casa, su casa."

"Thanks, Mom."

Cindy kicked off her heels, sat on the comfortable couch and cleared her throat. "Sit next to me, Mother."

Oh no. Mother, again. Now what?

I needed to sit for what came next.

"You must remember how I always wanted a bunch of relatives and how envious I was of all the kids in my class who had grandparents and cousins and aunts and uncles."

I wanted to cry. Yes. I'd never forgotten how deprived my little girl felt comparing how solitary her life was in comparison to all the other kids she knew. "Yes, I remember and I'll never forget how inadequate I felt at times but you had a wonderful dad and Rachel and dogs. I guess no toys or movies gave you what you needed to fill your heart. I'd stolen that from you by leaving home but Cindy, my parents forced me to leave when I got pregnant. They were ashamed of me and wanted me to give you up for adoption. So I ran away without telling the boy. We had just started dating and made a careless mistake. I certainly didn't want to force him to marry me and ruin his plans. We were only nineteen and he twenty one and both stupid." I took a breath, brushed away tears and held my stomach hoping the baby wouldn't feel my angst.

My precious daughter moved closer and embraced me. "Mom, I know your story, our story, and I've learned to understand. There's something I've never told you and, well, now's the time." Her blue eyes stared right into mine. "I tracked down my grandparents a long time ago when I took classes at law school. One class taught how to find people and I'm a quick learner, you know." I nodded, surprised and taken aback at the revelation. "They'd moved to an assisted living place in Florida because grandpapa had heart trouble and grandma couldn't take care of him alone."

Grandma. Grandpapa. Cindy spoke of the same people, my parents who'd thrown me out at nineteen, pregnant with money my grandfather left his only grandchild for her future. Instead I needed it to take care of a baby with hospital, doctors, shots, clothes, bills and a place to live. There was no end to it. I definitely had to depend on the kindness of strangers many times until that lucky day. Instead of my dream of becoming a veterinarian, I learned to groom animals How fortunate for me, for us to have landed in River's Edge and I found the perfect husband and father for my daughter. Choices. And now I looked at my daughter, a grown woman speaking of the same parents who cast us aside as if we were trash thirty plus years ago or more.

I paced the room. Drank water. Wanted to throw up. "So you're saying you've been in touch with them?"

She flinched. "Well, yes. For a long time."

"You realize they literally threw me out. They were disgusted and embarrassed by my uh, situation. That's what they called the pregnancy, Cindy. A situation. And you embrace them after that?"

"Mother, things were different back then. They're old and ill and sorry. I forgave them." Cindy held out her arms to me. I couldn't resist. I never could say no. That's me. "Open your big heart and remember good times. Think of our baby. We make choices, some good, some not so good. Do you regret having me?"

"Oh honey. Never. We always had each other. And don't you ever forget your father. Jim loved you as if you were his birth daughter."

"I know, Mom. I'll always love, Daddy Jim. But I've wondered forever about my other dad. What's his name, Mom?

She hadn't asked about him before. I pictured his face with high cheek bones and an almost square chin, curly blond hair like Cindy's, blue eyes like Cindy's, long and lean body. Again like Cindy. Even now my heart beat a little faster thinking of him. "His name is Scott Dwyer."

# Chapter Fifteen
# First Love

At work toward the end of one day, two months pregnant and feeling good I received a call from the nervous owner of a petulant poodle. As if I'm a dog whisperer she knew I could put the dog on a couch and solve her problems.

Taking full advantage of my preoccupation, my late day assistant Kathy in full make-up including extra lashes, whined about an aching back and left early tottering in spiked high heels. No pretending once Kathy opened the passenger door of yet another boyfriend's car. I'd find a replacement and give her notice tomorrow.

The day had passed in a furry flurry of dogs, big and small. Ready to wrap it up and lock the door, I heard the front door open and close. I smelled skunk! I yelled for the customer and the animal to hurry. "No time to waste. You strip, get your dog." I checked out the huge black German Shepherd. "What's his name?"

A deep voice said, "King."

"Tell King to get in the largest tub and you climb in with him. I'll get the tomato juice and together. Oh, just do it fast."

The voice gave a hand command to his pet and the royal dog cleared the edge of the tub and stood. K-9 training, I thought and almost spilled the open can of juice on my clothes. I caught a glimpse of powerful shoulders, a strong muscular frame and a great ass before he crouched next to King. "I read about a remedy created for skunk deodorizer and tried it. I can whip up another batch in a hurry but for now let's use up the tomato juice because," I paused to open another super size can, "my remedy contains peroxide and we must protect King's eyes. The ingredients are 1 Qt 3% hydrogen peroxide, ¼ cup baking soda, and 1teaspoon of liquid soap. King is large so he'll need a double batch. "

For the next fifteen concentrated minutes, the man and I poured rich red tomato juice over the quiet unmoving dog, working it through his coat After all eight cans were emptied, I told King's handler to come out and command King to STAY for just a bit longer. Turning my head away to give him privacy, I caught a glimpse of him in the mirror. At the same time our eyes met in a shock of recognition.

"Grace Meredith?"

"Guilty as charged. And is it really you, Scott Dwyer?"

"In the flesh." He grabbed a big towel and draped it around his waist. "Grace, you disappeared soon after we, uh, got together. Too much beer and marijuana back then, but I wanted to get to know you. I mean it. It wasn't like a one night thing, for me anyway. And then you were gone from school." He frowned. "I remember you planning to be a veterinarian."

"And of all the dog groomers in all the world, you walked into mine."

"Yeah. You loved Casablanca and you always made fun of yourself. So this is where you ended up."

The timer dinged. *The proverbial saved by the bell.* "King needs a good rinse right now." More conscious of my weight now that I'd seen Scott's body, I grabbed a big water proof smock and together we sluiced water all over the magnificent dog until the tomato red ran all clear. He shook himself dry, water spraying everywhere in the plastic covered area and then I gave him a sniff test to make sure an all clear skunk seal of approval meant good to go.

After me sneezing a few times, I gave a thumbs up to Scott. He toweled down his dog with gentle care and had me wishing *if only*. A pipe dream to nowhere.

"So you are with the police force?"

"Yeah. Captain Dwyer, here. K-9 is my specialty. Am I skunk free, too? Just asking since you applied the sniff test to my dog and I thought maybe."

"Maybe what?" Bedraggled, hair wet and straight, make-up gone from a day's work and then the skunk job. All in all, not a pretty sight and certainly not Grace from college days.

He beckoned to me. "Come a little closer, Grace. I won't bite. Promise."

"I bet you say that to all the dog groomers. Wait a minute. Are you married?" I saw a flicker of pain in his eyes. He shook his head. "Divorced, widower?" And I took a step closer.

Scott whispered, "Grace," and I pictured us in the stacks at the library, aflame with burning desire. "Oh, Grace. How long has it been?"

"About thirty six years." I knew because I was a naïve virgin and Cindy came from the wonderful times Scott and I were intimate.

We kissed, tentative at first and the hunger grew until I had no power to stop our awakened need for each other. He pulled back.

"Are you married?"

"I'm a widow.

"Oh. Were you married a long time?"

"Yes. He was a wonderful man, a realtor in town who became my partner in business here." I gestured to the shop.

"I have a small apartment upstairs. Come. Bring your dog and we'll catch up. My pooches are home with my housekeeper tonight. I'll call and ask her to stay a while longer." I hung my plastic smock on a hook to drip dry and walked upstairs. *Time to set the record straight. The baby I'm carrying is Scott's grandchild and he doesn't even know he has a daughter. Secrets. They catch up with you, Grace.*

To fill the silence, I babbled . "Coffee, tea, a drink?" Me, I really wanted to say and bit my tongue.

"Sit."

I sat and so did King. Scott and I burst into laughter. The command was for his dog and I obeyed. How goofy. Heat rushed to every part of my body. I still loved him.

"Fill me in, Grace."

Again we laughed. Fill me in the old expression before making love.

"Okay, you tell me why you ran away in 1960. Was it because you were pregnant and afraid to tell me?" I nodded. "Afraid our futures would be ruined because of a baby or what?"

"My parents disowned me and I," tears held in check for years trickled down, "and I feared you'd feel the same way so I ran."

"And we lost precious time, Grace but there's no going back. So you found your way to River's Edge eventually and began your grooming business and you married and made a good life here."

"Yes." He wiped away my tears. "And you? You married, became a police officer and now you're a widower." He nodded.

"Tell me about our child. What's his or her name, show me pictures, tell me everything."

"You don't have children?" Again I caught a fleeting flicker of pain.

He shook his head. "First our child."

"Please don't hate me for what I did. Running away and all."

"I promise. Life's too short and getting shorter by the minute."

"Her name is Cindy Scooter Trumbull."

"Scooter? Everyone called me Scooter."

I reached for the ever present album of my, our daughter. We poured over pictures from infancy through college graduation to winning her first law case. "She looks like me."

"Yes, she does. Blue eyes and curly blond hair where mine is straight." I touched my hair and face. "I'm a mess. Hair all straggly, no make-up and chubby. I must smell like dog after all the pets and then King's skunk attack."

King lifted his great head with straight pointed ears at the mention of his name. Scott gave him a biscuit and pointed to the floor. His magnificent dog chewed and settled down again.

Scott leaned over and sniffed my skin. "You're perfect."

I ran trembling fingers through his thick graying hair and inhaled his scent, no tomato juice or skunk remaining. Flustered I rose.

"Scott, I think we should have dinner and catch up before taking this to the next level."

He sighed. I saw disappointment and regret in his eyes. "You're right this time, Grace. But know this," he pulled me close, "this time we're not going to lose each other. No way." The steel in his voice rang with authority. *God, I loved him then and still love him.*

"Dinner here after I shower. You relax with King. Watch a movie, the news, read a book. Oh, keep yourself busy until I come out."

He laughed, King barked and I locked the bedroom and bathroom doors, hands shaking. *Get hold of yourself, Grace. He won't like a pregnant old lady.* After showering and drying my hair, I dressed in a loose outfit Cindy bought me. Ralph Lauren blue jean wide pants with a patterned shirt. I tied a silk scarf around my neck and thought the new me looked just fine.

"Your turn, Scott."

I found him thumbing through one of Cindy's albums again. This one had wedding pictures of me in a white lace tent dress and Jim and our friends laughing. He gazed up at me. "You're more beautiful now, Grace. Sit next to me and give me a timeline. Please. I want to know what became of you. Of us."

So I sat next to him. He sniffed my skin as if he wanted to inhale all of me. I didn't move for fear he'd notice my rounded shape and he turned pages. "After I wrote the stupid goodbye letter to you, the tenth draft, I drove all the way up to Buffalo to tell my parents what happened thinking they'd take care of me."

"Obviously they didn't."

"Right. Mother wanted me to have an abortion or give the baby away so I turned around and drove not knowing where to go until I stopped and met a nice Doctor who confirmed the pregnancy and gave me pre natal vitamins and I drove on until another good person gave me directions to River's Edge and."

"You met a lot of kind people. On the other hand, a girl alone, terrible things can happen."

"They didn't. I drove into town, went to a realtor and met Jim, married him," I pointed to the goofy picture and told him about how the Pet Emporium became a partnership venture, "and Scott, Jim was forty when we married and happy to be Cindy's father. I was this lost kid trying to find my way and I did. With his support and authority in town. We had a good life."

I rose, grabbed his hand and pushed him toward the shower. "Clean up while I make dinner. Then I want to know all about you."

The fridge didn't offer a great selection so I called my favorite take out and by the time Scott came out smelling just the way I did, the doorbell rang. "Tucci's Italian here to serve you, Grace." King stood on the alert. I called for Scott. A K-9 dog listens only to his handler. Scott gave a command and King obeyed rewarded with a biscuit while I paid Georgio, my special delivery boy. "Thanks for good fast service."

"No cooking here?"

"No food here. Not today. Set the table for a feast." I unwrapped a quarter of a chicken breast with mushrooms and spinach for me and two whopping lasagna slices for Scott with a salad for two complete with olives, hearts of Romaine, tomato slices, slivers of red onion, and crisp croutons. Dressing on the side.

I lit two candles and we sat opposite each other. I wanted to jump his bones before and after dinner. "Bon appétit." Eating slowly, I watched Scott wondering what his life had been the past thirty five years and knew I had to wait 'til after dinner.

"This is delicious, Grace. Do you order in often?"

"If you're asking do I entertain gentlemen callers up her, the answer is no. Not ever. Sometimes when my staff and I are too pressured to stop for lunch, we'll call and Marconi's delivers. It's a family owned business like many in River's Edge. Where do you live?"

He rolled his shoulders to relax them, a motion I recalled from the few months we were together.. "Rockland County. Pearl River. It's a big town, the largest enclave of Irish in the States." He grinned. "The St. Patrick's Day parade is something to behold."

We finished dinner; he fed King and walked him while I wondered what to do when they returned. The question was answered when they came up the stairs and King lay down. Scott and I sat on the couch and swapped stories about past years.

"What brought you up to this neck of northern New York?"

He stretched his long legs, ankles crossed and half smiled showing a dimple in his cheek. "I have time off and decided to check out the place where there are waterfalls and streams I've heard about. Also I wanted a place where King could roam free for a while." He shook his head, a blond lock of hair falling across his forehead. "Bad mistake. That's where King met skunk and skunk won." Suddenly he pulled me in his

89

arms and we kissed. Years peeled away but this time I could say no.

"No, Scott. Not yet. Tell me more. Tell me everything and I'll tell you so we can fill in the blanks."

"Okay, but stay close or I'll come after you again." *Oh how I wanted to.* "And if King hadn't lost the battle today, I never would have found you. Was it a chance encounter? I don't think so, Grace. Meant to be is more like it." *Silently I agreed.* "1960. You broke my heart by disappearing and I graduated without knowing where you'd gone or why. Everyone partied hard so I made an attempt to join my buddies, drank too much and staggered back to the dorm, packed up and went home to my folks. I did get your parents phone number in Buffalo. You father seemed bewildered about your whereabouts and your mother hung up."

"A far cry from the house with the picket fence and lots of relatives."

Another kiss. "You remember. I didn't know where else to look. If I'd been a cop back then, I'd have put out an APB and found you hiding in plain sight."

*He came close,* I thought, *but no cigar and here we were, no longer kids, in our fifties. Between the two of us, we'd racked up a lot of mileage.*

"Cuddle up. I'll reveal all if you will."

"Not a good idea, Scott."

"Hmm. Okay, I'll peel off a layer first and then it's your turn. How's that for a plan?" He nudged me in the ribs just missing my expanding middle. "Like, uh, peeling an onion."

"Or strip poker."

"Even better." His eyes sparkled with enthusiasm just like in the old days.

"I agree on my terms. We have thirty five years to cover. You give me five first."

"One kiss before?"

"No way." I scooted across to the end of the couch and settled in, a pillow across my middle.

"Down, boy." I knew it wasn't King he spoke to. The magnificent animal snored on a rug next to the door.

He appeared to search in some distant place before beginning and then the words poured out. "After graduation, I went to Yale Law planning on law toward an FBI future like so many feds. Finally I decided on John Jay University in NYC for all studies connected with law enforcement. It was a new school, very exciting and I fit in and began to make choices."

"Choices?"

"Yeah. Which direction to take and then," he paused and his enthusiastic expression changed, "I met Pamela Cartwright. And what attracted me to Pam, you might ask?" I shrugged as if I didn't have a clue and I didn't. "She was petite, like you, with silky dark brown hair, like yours. That's where the resemblance ended. We married. Busy with studies and long hours, I didn't realize she drank. A lot. Vodka. And only stopped when she got pregnant. Scott Junior was two months old in a car bed in the back seat of our two-door Ford when she drove to the store one night." His sad blue eyes looked across the couch, across the years, to find mine. One swift move brought me to his side.

"Driving home I passed an accident. Like all the other stupid drivers, I slowed. The car was a dark blue Ford like the one Pam drove. Something inside me said to pull over. A cop waved me along and then he recognized me and came over. I asked him what happened.

"Oh Geez," he said. "Nasty and tragic. This lady slammed into a truck doing seventy miles an hour. She's dead and so," Scott choked on tears, "and so is the baby. They were thrown from the car on impact." My long lost love sat quiet and finished. "I knew without looking I'd lost my baby boy and my sick wife."

We held each other for a long time. Down Main Street the town clock chimed ten; birds roosting there scattered in a flapping of wings. Life went on as if nothing had happened in the apartment above the Pet Emporium. After a while I caressed his face and placed his hand on my belly. "Here's some interesting news for you."

He did that familiar tilt of his head so dear to me. "After my first five years of revelation to you, I hope it's an improvement."

"Our daughter, Cindy Scooter Adler, has had infertility problems for a long time and she and her husband Len, you'll love them both, have asked me to be surrogate for their baby."

He frowned. "I don't understand."

"In simple words, I'm going to carry their baby for them."

"What?"

"Yes. And right now I'm two months pregnant with your grandchild."

"Oh. Oh. Oh." His hand caressed my rounding abdomen over and over again. "You mean in here is our grandbaby?"

"Yes. Oh yes." King lifted his great head as if sensing something momentous was going on. The whole idea of sharing the news with Scott curled my socks like the first time he kissed me except I wasn't wearing any socks. I felt like a kid again and didn't say no when gently he led me into the bedroom. Removing my loose sweater turned out to be no problem since I aided and abetted my cop with every move. *And how come it ended just like in days of old with me sans clothing and Scott still dressed?*

"Well what do we have here?"

At least I smelled good, we both used the same body wash an hour before. Naked I certainly wasn't the skinny virgin when he first saw me sans clothing. I made a feeble attempt to cover up.

"Hey, it's just me, Grace, plus thirty five years of wear and tear. What you see is what you get. No returns this time. You are a fragile orchid, my love. I'll never let you go."

"Good. Fragile, huh? No bungee jumping or bouncing on a trampoline this time around?"

"Nope."

With sweet may I do this? and how about that? Scott and I made it through to the grand finale of love making without damage. Holding hands and catching our respective breaths afterward, Scott asked me to marry him.

"You want to make an honest woman of me, do you?"

"It's about time, don't you think?"

"I think. Tomorrow I'll call our daughter so you can meet her before the wedding."

# Chapter Sixteen

Saturday, we cleaned up and trudged downstairs before the staff arrived. Scott crossed the street to pick up breakfast I'd ordered at Mimi's Diner. After he left to return, she called. "You have a new boyfriend, Grace? He's adorable."

"He's slightly used, Mimi. We met in college and got reacquainted last night. By chance."

"Tell me more."

"Not now but Mimi, here's a head's up, he's going to be around from now on." I hung up.

I smelled pancakes the minute he walked in the door. King was out in back on the dog walk so we dined, laughing over nothing. He paced the Emporium waiting for me to call Cindy.

"Honey, are you and Len busy this morning? I have something important to discuss with you. Maybe around noon?"

"Oh Mom, are you okay? Nothing is wrong with the baby, right?"

"Not to worry. I'm fine. Are you free at noon or later today?"

"Just a sec, I'll ask Len." She returned a few minutes later. "Noon is the best time for us. See you then." I heard panic in her voice. My girl. Always in a rush to fix whatever might be going wrong. This time she was in for a big surprise. I chuckled and reached for a smock. Petra and Mike showed up with Johnny and Marge close behind. Customers were already pulling into parking spaces.

I introduced Scott to everyone and noticed the women giving him sideways glances. Definitely a hunk, my guy.

"What can I do to help?

"First take care of King. Then when he's settled down come watch the operation here. We're very organized and we keep the flow of pets moving along with efficiency and a lot of love. If there's a special needs dog, I take over and have a chat with the animal."

"You talk to them to heal them?"

"Yes. It's a gift. I don't know where it came from and I don't question it but they improve. Usually it's personality."

"Hmm." He kissed me as if it were an everyday occurrence and went off to care for King.

The morning passed quickly. I felt Scott's presence behind me as he watched and soon, out of the corner of my eye, I saw him roll up his sleeves and join in whenever someone needed a helping hand.

The BMW pulled up in front and Cindy flew out of the car to enter my shop. She looked around to find me washing my hands. "You're all right!"

"I said I was fine, honey. Bring Len in."

Len raced in and hugged me. "Thank God you're okay, Mom."

"Kids, there's someone I want you to meet. Come upstairs." I beckoned to Scott. His face turned red. I felt his nervousness across the shop. "There's a K-9 trained dog in the apartment. His handler is right behind us. Let him go first." Scott rushed by, entered and spoke to King. We came in.

I spoke rapidly, words pouring out nonstop on one breath."Cindy, this is Scott Dwyer, your birth father. We talked about him the other night and by chance,"

She interrupted me. "I look like you. Oh my God. Len, do you see what I see? It's a miracle. Can I touch you to see if you're real?"

Scott opened his arms and hugged his daughter for the first time. "It is a miracle."

I sat in the old rocking chair and rocked to clear away the anxiety felt before this joyous meeting. Len and I were bystanders for the moment. Bursting with our personal news, I couldn't contain myself anymore. "Scott and I have decided to get married."

"Oh." Cindy's face changed from joy and she frowned. "But what would Dad think?"

"Cindy, he'd want me to be happy again and meeting Scott is a bonus like winning the lottery."

King growled. Scott gave him a command. "So I'm a bonus, huh? Like winning the lottery. You have a way with words, my Grace." He kissed me and turned to the kids. "I'm a lawyer so we begin with a lot in common."

"You are?" Cindy grinned and looked like a little kid. *My daughter, so mercurial.*

"Yes. I went to Yale thinking FBI and ultimately finished studies at John Jay in NYC. I told your mom all about my past, at least the first five years after we lost touch. She still has to fill me in about her first five. This might take the rest of our lives. Meanwhile, we're having a baby and I'll be with her every step of the way." He tweaked my nose. "No chocolates, young lady. The best healthy food and afterward, we splurge."

"And you're in law enforcement now?" Len jumped in, his intelligent eyes sparkling.

"I'm ready to retire. I'm an officer in the K-9 Corp, narcotic and criminal detection. King is my partner." King barked his approval.

While we lunched at Mimi's in my favorite booth in a far corner, I tackled yet another grilled chicken breast, salad with squeezed lemon for taste. My family made plans for me as if I had no choice in the matter. At this point, I didn't care. Scott and I would marry fast before I'd begin to waddle; he'd accompany me to the nice doctor. *Funny how life changed so quickly. Just because a skunk had his way with King. And no* longer would Doctor Ingersol be the only man familiar with my private parts. I have Scott. My main man.

"What's so amusing, Grace? Is there something in the salad I should know about?"

"Just stuff. Life." I leaned over to kiss him and share my lemon flavored tongue.

"Not in front of the children, dear."

"They better get married fast. Mom's getting nutsy, Len."

"I can see that."

# Chapter Seventeen

Scott's family had lined up on a long covered porch. *Like a Norman Rockwell painting,* I thought. The white picket fence he'd described when we met in 1960 still there but what a spread of land to encompass. My BMOC came from not so modest a background. Smiles and waves came from all sizes of relatives. At last Cindy and I had it all.

I wanted a simple ceremony. Scott agreed and said his mother had a plan. "Not to worry, honey," he said. "Buy a pretty dress," he said. "Just some friends and family," he said.

"Tell your mom. No gifts. Make a donation for rescue shelters. Um. Just write a check or leave cash and I'll make sure the money goes where it's needed. And I'll send a receipt. We don't need a toaster."

So I bought a wide skirted print summer dress guaranteed to camouflage my middle and white three inch heels and a big floppy straw hat. Perfect for a second hand bride. Scott intended to wear his uniform one last time.

"Are there any more guests coming?" I clutched Scott's hand before all the blond curly headed people who looked a lot like him surged toward us.

"Not to worry, sweetheart. Just a few. Mom had a plan and today's the day you're mine."

His words stayed with me as we were swamped with hugs and kisses. "You've finally found each other. It's a miracle, isn't it, Dad." Lydia, my mother-in-law beamed.

Scott's dad peered over his glasses. "Yes, dear."

I said, "Good answer." All the kids laughed

An hour later I was not prepared for the arrival of fellow officers from Scott's unit, my gang from the Emporium, Mimi from the Diner, and colleagues from Trumbull Realtors.

Cindy stood next to a very old couple; a man in a wheelchair and an elderly woman obviously dressed with care. She waved for me to come over as soon as I could. Scott guided me, made introductions. Lots of handshakes and kisses. Me careful to watch out for too close enthusiastic hugging with Scott in protective mode.

As I approached Cindy and the old folks, my fists clenched. Mother and father withered with age come to. *To what? Bizarre*, I thought. *A Kafka scene of horror on my wedding day. Then I recalled Cindy's story of how she tracked them down years ago and how terrible they felt about the way they treated me. Relax. Calm down. Forgive and let go. A baby is coming and you have Scott.*

After taking a deep breath, I greeted my parents, touched their trembling hands and thanked them for coming. Cindy's smile rewarded my generosity of the moment. I never claimed to be saintly. Just older and wiser like our vows.

"They're going to stay long enough to see the ceremony and afterward they'll fly back to Florida. I hope you don't mind, Mom."

I never could resist my daughter. She wanted family and now her dreams were coming true. "It's fine, honey. I have to ask, do I look all right? Scott didn't tell me his mother wanted him to have a big wedding. He said I should buy a summer dress so I did."

She hugged me the way I'd always done to her through the years. "You are the cutest bride, Mom."

*Hmm. Cute? At my age. Oh well. Today anything goes.*

With a light breeze blowing and the scent of honeysuckle all around, we walked down a makeshift aisle covered by a red carpet toward the Justice of the Peace. A four piece band played "I Can't Stop Lovin' You," our favorite song from 1960. He had the power to pronounce us husband and wife. We had our vows spoken together. "We lost and finally found each other thirty five years later. Fate stepped in and here we are a bit wiser, definitely older, and ready to last forever. That's us. Scott and Grace."

Cheers erupted when we kissed. I didn't hear anyone whisper, "Oh look, she's pregnant." So far so good.

The Dwyer clan spared no expense with an elaborate wedding feast. Striped umbrellas and white table cloths gave the huge yard a festive appearance. Waiters carried trays and offered succulent snacks before the carving began. A chef complete with hat and sparkling white jacket stepped out with a fanfare and dinner was officially served as the sky turned pink to blend with blue and soft billowing clouds made their way across the sky. The band hit Twist and Shout, friends danced and I watched, stirring a few shrimp around my plate. I longed to dance and waited for slower music. We waved off the first dance for bride and groom tradition. Scott whispered. "Are you all right, my wife?"

"Yes. I just didn't expect such a fuss. Um. It's such an extravagant affair."

"Grace, my family has waited for years to see me happy. When I told them I'd found you and we were going to get married right away, they insisted on..." he gestured to the lights, umbrellas, waiters, everything, "I couldn't turn them down. So let's enjoy every moment. You have a big family now, my Grace. Loner no more. And they don't know about our Cindy and our grandbaby." His hand slipped under my dress. I stopped him before anyone noticed.

"Down, boy." We laughed. "Let's slow dance in a little while. We also have to mingle. Not my favorite thing." I noticed Cindy and Len were like politicians doing a meet and greet with poise.

He stood to greet friends from his unit. And took a ribbing over the old guy getting married. I chimed in, "Who said old? You'll have to arm wrestle me for that comment." I made a muscle showing strength from years of lifting dogs and grooming.

"My wife, men. Don't cross Grace Dwyer. She's tough." He kissed the top of my head.

One of the guys said, "What about King? How's he acclimating to the change in venue."

"Grace has King eating out of her hand. I said she's tough and smart. In River's Edge they call her the dog whisperer."

I smacked my husband on the shoulder. "Enough, sweetheart." Pointing to the bar, "I said, "Men, if you're looking around, I do believe you might find some single women over there." They sauntered away toward greener pastures.

Scott pulled me into a full body, gentle embrace complete with a hot kiss leaving me breathless. The gathering clanked cutlery against glasses wanting more. We danced then, no fast moves or turns, just ballroom. "Nice." I snuggled under his chin. "So nice."

*Am I being so careful because of the baby and my age? Yes. At fifty-four I can't bop around like a teen. Sorry, old girl.*

After thanking Scott's parents, so strong and healthy in their seventies, and waving goodbye and see you soon, we drove home to River's Edge where we'd decided to live in my old home in the woods. After much discussion and taking real estate values into account, why move when we might renovate to our own taste? A sensible idea and we needed a playroom for Junior and our growing canine family. King hadn't met my mini poodles so there were adjustments to be made. We talked all the way home 'til we reached the Emporium where my friend, Annie, a trained handler, stayed in my apartment with King.

They were out in the yard where Annie threw a ball and King raced and caught it every time. We watched through the window and then joined them. King stopped. Scott used his high pitched voice to command King to come. He galloped to his master, his best pal, Scott. Then he came to me and offered his big paw as if to shake in greeting. I almost cried. Our dog. I stroked his big head way back to his tail over and over, deep into the fur to let know I love him.

"How did he do, Annie? Was he much trouble?"

"No. We have a thing going. He ate well and slept well. It was only overnight, Scott. But I'd do it again anytime. He's a good boy."

"Tell that to drug dealers he's helped bring in over the years. Anyway, thanks. How much do we owe you?"

She shook her head. "Grace has been very generous to me through the years. I'm happy to return her kindness. Hey Grace, when's the baby due?"

Caught! "How do you know?"

"Geez, Grace. Everyone in town knows. I'm a mom. I knew right away. Just something about a preggers. Well, God Bless and good luck. It's not easy when you're uh, how old?"

"Annie, get out before I spank you and you know I'm tough enough to do just that. Thanks for taking care of King and hush about me, you hear!" The door closed. Annie's laughter carried in the still night air.

"Scott, our secret is out!"

"No, honey. Forget about it. One day at a time. Now I'll get King's bed and food, pack my bag and we'll move into our new home. Tomorrow I go with you to the doctor and tell him not to peek."

*Oh baby. I'm in for a fun filled time. A husband who doesn't want the doctor to look at my privates, is he kidding or what? The whole town knows I'm with child, and NO CHOCOLATE.* I laughed all the way home.

Laughing no more when King met my miniature poodles, Prince and Princess. They came up to the first joint in his hind quarter. "I'll handle this." Scott assured me he had control of a

103

delicate situation. My dogs, their domain. King, the interloper. A huge scary interloper.

The command to stay didn't help for long when my little guys sniffed all around the mountainous creature. King joined in the sniffing party, seemed to approve of the small critters at his feet and gave a lick that knocked Princess over. A game began; a lick then a roll over and bounce back of small acrobatic poodles.

We stepped back and laughed ready to intercede in case of danger. Finally my man walked, watered, and fed them all and spread King's bed out near the front door Scott and I went up the stairs to honeymoon, carefully.

# Chapter Eighteen

Dr. Ingersol looked up perplexed. "I hear two heart beats. One must have been hiding behind the other. This is not good news for a surrogate your age."

"What?" Scott and I said at the same time."You mean twins are in there?"

"Yes. And Grace, you must make a decision to um, only have one."

Scott almost grabbed the nice doctor by the throat. "You mean kill one baby?"

"Mr. Dwyer, I realize you're intense about this grandchild but it's wiser for Grace to carry one. For her health and for the baby. Think about it. I'll be right back." The doctor ran for his life as far I could tell.

"Calm down honey. We'll research the problem and make a rational decision. Personally for a healthy specimen like me, I'm not in favor of selective termination. It sounds so, uh Nazi like."

"No, Grace, it's for health reasons when necessary. We'll listen to Doctor Ingersol and get Cindy and Len over for a consultation. If this means you have to have bed rest, take it easy, off your feet, it's only for a few more months. Let's get him back here and listen. I'm sorry I went ballistic."

The doctor returned. I had dressed and we sat at in his office and tried to appear calm. As if we dropped in for tea.

Scott apologized for flying off the handle. The doctor accepted. All very civilized. "Please explain possibilities and consequences so we can make a decision, Dr. Ingersol."

After clearing his throat, the doctor said, "There's a risk to you, Grace because of your age. Carrying twins is not easy at any age. If you do carry both of them, you may very well require bed rest, absolutely no sexual activity, and most likely an early delivery. Pregnancy is difficult at best. Your situation doubles the precariousness of the situation. And you must consult with your daughter and her husband before a final decision. That said," he folded his hands, "you are in remarkable good health. That's a plus." He rose. Our little talk had ended.

We rode down in the elevator holding hands. "Time for a family Pow Wow. Carry me to the car, big guy."

A little humor goes a long way. At home, I called Cindy. "Hi honey, we just got back from the doctor."

"And what did he say. How are you?"

"We've got double trouble and need you and Len to come over for a conference."

"Double?" She shrieked. "Twins? We'll be there in an hour." She hung up.

Meanwhile, Scott fed the dogs that got along as if they were all the same size, and booted up the computer. Time to check on older surrogates who delivered twins. He muttered singles, singles, singles, and suddenly Eureka as if he'd discovered fire. "I've got a hit on one woman from Australia who carried for her son's wife and delivered twins a year ago. All of them are healthy. And here's another in New Zealand who successfully had twins at fifty three. So far it's good, Grace."

I moaned. "Find someone in New York so I can talk to her." I whined. "I'm hungry."

"Me too. Warm up the lasagna from last night and I'll broil salmon for you with risotto rice." I knew right away my husband would not pamper me unless he felt it absolutely necessary.

By the time the kids arrived, we were settled down and ready to discuss a complex situation.

Cindy and Len, on the other hand, arrived rattled and fearful.

"What have we gotten you into, Mom?" Cindy cried. Scott gave her a command worthy of a K-9 hostage situation.

"Let's approach this rationally or Grace and I will decide without your histrionics." She stopped the floodgate of tears. "We are against selective termination and feel the best solution, since your mother is in good health for any age, is for her to allow her assistants to do the heavy lifting at The Emporium. She can continue with her dog whisperer amazing talents and stay off her feet as needed. As the babies grow, I'll assume more work. Already I've learned some grooming techniques and will continue. We'll have full time help at home and Dr. Ingersol will keep a close watch on her progress."

He held me in his arms as if that would protect me for the months to come. *Maybe it would all work out,* I thought. *Wishful thinking taken to a new level.*

Scott said, "You're up."

They appeared to be stunned as they glanced at each other and stared at us. We had made the decision before they arrived. Len began. "The most important factor is Mom's health. We've prayed for a baby for five years and suddenly it's complicated. We don't want to lose one."

"Or the other." Cindy sat on the floor and touched our hands. "Let's do what you've said, Dad and pray for the best." After a long silence, she stood and made chamomile tea. "Any chocolate chip cookies around here, Mom?"

"No caffeine until after the births. There are some cookies in the pantry. Enough for three. I'll have some raisins. Oh yummy."

I shut my ears to their talk about older surrogates in far off lands who had twins. *Enough already. Go home and leave* me alone with a good book and our dogs. No sex and no chocolate. Five months to go and who's counting. What a life.

# Chapter Nineteen

Singing "The falling leaves drift by my window. . ." was an optimistic way to begin the day. I pictured Doris Day singing the song, hitting every note, me a teenager straining for the high notes and giving up. I switched to "And the days dwindle down to a precious few," feeling the bump, kicks, and roll of kids one and two responding to the music. I patted my belly and hoped they'd calm down.

"Scott, will you still love me with a scar on my belly after the C section?"

"No." He came close to me and lifted my once baggy tee shirt, now stretched to capacity. Warm strong hands spread across to measure the width and girth of me. Fingers did a stealthy march to the dark moist of me. "I want to love you like I've never loved you before. Right now."

"Oh, Scooter. Lie down and let me satisfy you until this is over. It won't be much longer. Maybe a month. Yes. One more month and they'll be cooked. A C section is over without the pain and hours of labor."

After the loving of my good man, we lay together eyes closed until I felt a sharp kick way down low. I didn't like the feeling at all. "Scott, call the Doctor and get me to the hospital right now."

He made the call, carried me out the door and we were off. Dr. Ingersol and his best staff were there waiting as Scott pushed the wheelchair into the emergency room. After close examination, the good doctor looked grim. "Let's do a section right now. She's going into labor."

"Doctor, is there a way to stop labor and give the babies a chance to stay where they are for a little longer?"

Dr. Ingersol looked at my husband for one long moment as if who was this moron to challenge my judgment. Then a different expression crossed his face. "There is an old fashioned method we can try. It's worth a chance for maybe a half day." Briskly he ordered a drip for me, something saline, I couldn't make out what he said.

Scott squeezed my hand. The process began. Throughout the day, I dozed, and Scott, ever vigilant, stayed at my side. The doctor came in and smiled after listening to my insides. "Ah. Very good. Thanks, Mr. Dwyer. Have you had previous experience?"

"Yes. As an officer in the K-9 Corp for many years, you come across many situations and I remembered a woman we found going into labor prematurely and one of the cops in my unit called a medic who did exactly what you just accomplished. And not in the cleanest environment."

I heard what sounded like a mutual sigh of relief. "We'll keep Grace here for a few days to monitor her. After this scare, if she can hang in for a month, we're home free."

"Bite your tongue, Doc. We'll do the best we can."


Don't alarm the kids became our motto. Whenever Cindy called, like five times a day, Scott said I was fine. Or I answered and chirped, "Cool, not to worry."

Four days later, I went home. We agreed it was a close call. Three weeks more to go. The forecast called for snow. It started with a light dusting. We laughed watching the dogs frolic in the yard we finally fenced in for safety.

"It's gonna be a big one." The jolly weatherman carried on from his warm studio and pointed to an unreadable screen of snow, rain and more across the northern eastern part of the US. At this time we weren't interested in what was going on anywhere else. Scott piled wood inside and set the fire blazing with tight twisted newspaper as kindling. Feet up on an ottoman, I sighed and hoped today was not the day.

Warning came during the height of the storm. Pain radiated across my lower back enough to scare both of us to get moving and fast. Light snowflakes became a blizzard when Scott, once again, phoned the doctor and windshield wipers going like a runaway metronome, drove me to the emergency room. This time Dr. Ingersol rushed us to the fourth floor for delivery. My husband's face pinched with worry. "I love you, Sweetheart. See you and the kids in a few."

This time, full of confidence, I put myself in the nice doctor's hands and used yoga breathing exercises to help relax. I visualized palm trees, a beach with waves lapping at the shore to create my own space and only half listened to preparations and the speed as my doctor worked to take my grandchildren from me and bring them into the world.

A healthy cry from baby one rang out followed by a softer squeal from baby two a few minutes later. "Grace, they look perfect." Dr. Ingersol spoke to me, his voice had a satisfied sound to it. "Your grandson weighed in at four pounds, two ounces and his sister topped the scale at four pounds even. They have curly blond hair like their mother." He leaned over and spoke softly. "I'm so proud of you. For what you've accomplished as my oldest surrogate and the care you've taken to help make this happen."

"Ask Scott to come in and I really need some dark chocolate."

He chuckled. "Your husband's on his way but no chocolate until later. Please." He patted my foot. *I wondered why the hell doctors do that. Doctoring 101?*

"Did you see our kids?"

Tears ran down his face. "I couldn't be with you for our daughter's birth but here we are with two grandkids. Grace, we'll be the best grandparents ever."

"Honey, I've heard the best thing about being a grandparent is that you don't have to pay for their education and when they visit and go home, you wave bye-bye and the house is quiet again."

We both glanced over at the baskets where the babies slept. Swaddled in blue and pink, little knitted caps on their heads, tiny fists curled, they were delicious. Cindy and Len arrived to go nuts over their newborns. The Palisade Parkway was in progress of being cleared and they had to follow a snowplow most of the way from New York City. They were allowed five minutes to see the twins and after hugs to me, Scott, Cindy and Len went down to the cafeteria. Peace at last. I slept until a nurse came in.

"The room reserved for Mr. and Mrs. Len Adler is ready."

"They might be in the coffee shop. Please page them." I'd forgotten in all the rush they'd stay for a few days to learn how to care for the babies from a special nurse. They had hired someone a while ago and she'd live-in for a few months and probably longer since my daughter was a lawyer. As far as I knew, Cindy had already enrolled them in nursery school, dance, music lessons, and computer classes. And maybe Law School. I'd have to convince her to let them be kids for a long time first.

With that happy thought, I closed my eyes and dreamed of sex and dark chocolate, in that order.

The Beginning. . .Not The End

# More Great Books by Charmaine Gordon

**ALSO IN AUDIOBOOK!**

The first three stories in the series of Mature Romance combined in one volume. Instant Grandpa, Book 1; Young at Heart, Book 2; and Before the Final Curtain, Book 3. These Charmaine Gordon stories of love, passion, and suspense starring sexy seniors are also available as singles in ebook.

## *Instant Grandpa, Book 1*

Summer at the Jersey Shore just got hotter... Take one widower grandfather, add two little grandkids, and widowed grandmother with a small granddaughter. Mix well. Stir in sun drenched beach days and moonlit nights. What have you got? A kite flying high with a new tail; an author writing a book to sort out emotions; a talented boy with his mother returned to claim the prize.

## Young at Heart , Book 2

Seventy year old Joyce Campbell expected her new left hip to heal at Helen Hayes Rehabilitation. What she didn't expect was to fall in love with the distinguished silver haired Collin Brody who wouldn't give her a second glance. Until Kizzy, the therapy dog comes into Collin's life...and into his heart. What happens next? The Beginning, Not the End.

## Before the Final Curtain, Book 3

Once lovers, aging actors collide on stage as stars in a romantic comedy written and directed by a manipulative director. Add to the mix the talented assistant, a tough stage manager, one prominent costume designer, two young actors, secrets and gossip. Show business. There's no business like it.

## No Time for Green Bananas

*The Beginning, Not the End*, Book 4

Celeste Hamlin, seventy-five year old widow, has a goal... conquer the six mountains in the Saranac Lake region before deciding what to do with the rest of her life.

Sixty-two year old Professor Paul Harris, meets the dynamic Celeste, and recalls the last words his wife said before she passed. "Find another love and begin again." Will they begin again?

### *The Catch*

Tom Donnelly, once known as The Catch – every woman's dream guy, has fallen down every rung of the ladder he once worked so hard to climb. On New Year's Day, he realizes just how far he's fallen, and makes a list of resolutions to change his life. He vows to regain the trust lost from his family, his law firm, and his friends – and maybe even find the right woman this time.

### *Sin of Omission*

A twist of fate intervenes when Shelley keeps a secret that threatens to break apart the Costigans and her future. A mysterious client, Deanna Rose, enters Haven, victim of a savage beating under strange circumstances. Shelley investigates and finds Ms. Rose has an unsavory past. With the reputation and safety of Haven at stake, Shelley is at risk to lose everything and everyone she cares about.

### *Reconstructing Charlie*

Charlie Costigan has a secret. Home life gone from bad to the worst when she protects her mother from another vicious attack by her drunken father. Midnight. Clothes thrown into an old suitcase, she races for the bus with a letter to an unknown aunt and uncle. "This is my daughter. Embrace her as if she were your own." Determined, Charlie begins again. Alone with her secret.

### *Now What?*

I held his cooling hand and asked the two words spoken many times during our years together. "Now what?" This time there was no response. I was on my own for the first time. When my fingers touched his wedding ring, I slipped it off and held it in my fist. The gold band was warm. I clung to him. "Come back to me, dearest." Sometimes what you wish for is more than you can live with.

### *Starting Over*

Each morning, Emily Kendrick runs on the hard-packed sand of St. Augustine Beach to clear her mind and heal her heart. From the widow's walk of the house perched high on the dunes, a man trains his binoculars on Emily...

 **ALSO IN AUDIOBOOK! OPTIONED FOR TELEVISION MOVIE!**

### *To Be Continued*

Elizabeth Malone wakes up the morning after an amazing night of passion with her husband of forty years to find a note: Dear Lizzie, it's not you, it's me. Abandoned by her husband, disappointed in daughter Susie's casual attitude Dad's having a mid-life crisis, Beth decides to re-establish herself as the winner she once was. When Frank Malone returns, he's in for a big surprise!

**Charmaine Gordon** writes books about women who Survive and Thrive. Her motto is take one step and then another to leave your past behind and begin again. Six books and several short stories in three years, she's always at work on the next story. The books include *To Be Continued, Starting Over, Now What?, Reconstructing Charlie, Sin of Omission* and *The Catch*, and her series of Mature Romances, The Beginning...Not the End.

"I didn't realize at the time while working as an actor in NYC, I'd become a sponge soaking up dialogue, setting, and stage directions. I learned many tools of writing during the years watching directors like Mike Nichols and actors including Harrison Ford, Anthony Hopkins, and Billy Crystal. And would you believe, I was Geraldine Ferraro's stand-in leg model, my first job giving me entrée into all the Unions needed to work. When the sweet time ended, I began another career and creative juices flowed."

You can reach Charmaine at
http://authorCharmaineGordon.wordpress.com

And on her FB page
http://www.facebook.com/charmaine.gordon

www.ingramcontent.com/pod-product-compliance
Lightning Source LLC
Chambersburg PA
CBHW060644130626
46555CB00002B/954